DESSIE D. MOORE

Keisha on the Case

iUniverse, Inc.
Bloomington

iUniverse books may be ordered through booksellers or by contacting:

iUniverse
1663 Liberty Drive
Bloomington, IN 47403
www.iuniverse.com
1-800-Authors (1-800-288-4677)

Because of the dynamic nature of the Internet, any Web addresses or links
contained in this book may have changed since publication and may no longer be
valid. The views expressed in this work are solely those of the author and do not
necessarily reflect the views of the publisher, and the publisher hereby disclaims
any responsibility for them.

ISBN: 978-1-4502-6037-4 (sc)
ISBN: 978-1-4502-6036-7 (ebook)

Printed in the United States of America

iUniverse rev. date: 10/25/2010

Prologue

My Grandma Flora used to say that there ain't no stranger story than a true one. I wish she had been around when this strange story took place and changed my life. Grandma was a very smart woman; she would have known what to do. Maybe she would have kept me out of trouble?

My story, well really our story, begins on a regular day. Simply ordinary in fact.

Picture this: Sunshine on a beautiful white and yellow kitchen; the smell of turkey bacon and eggs filling the room. Enter player no.1, (also known as the person who gets me involved in this mess in the first place) Jamal Lewis. His mother was at the stove humming under her breath as she put the last touch on perfectly scrambled eggs. She wore a pretty blue dress and a gloriously white apron, nails and lipstick were perfectly done and bright red. Jamal must have made a sound because his mother turned to greet him.

"Good morning hon."

"Uh," was all Jamal could manage.

"Sit down, and have your breakfast. After all, it's the most important meal of the day." Jamal's knees began to shake and he flopped down into the chair across from his Dad, who was happily smoking his pipe and reading the morning paper.

"Says here it's going to be another beautiful day, Mother."

"That's nice dear."

"I think I'll wear my blue sweater, so my sweetheart and I will match like two peas in a pod."

"Oh, honey, that's so sweet." She leaned over the paper in order to kiss him in the center of his forehead. He began to play with the long straight locks of hair while they gazed into each others eyes as if they were the only two people in the world.

Jamal began to make choking noises, and two pairs of concerned eyes turned in his direction.

"Son, are you okay?" The voice was his father's; the eyes were his father's. But something was wrong. He nodded and the two watchers went back to making breakfast and reading the paper in the center of a smoky haze. The happy pair continued to joke and play all through breakfast. Beautiful golden sunlight continued to shine in through the kitchen window, the appliances were as clean as they'd been before, although now it seemed sinister - somehow watchful and dangerous. These two people had eyes only for each other, so no one saw the tears as they rolled down the face of one very confused young man

Chapter 1

This is where the story really begins to get interesting. This is where I come in. I'm Keisha. You know, Keisha Johnson? Oh, well, never mind, I'm just an ordinary 13 year old from Oceanside, California. My home is the apartment on Dubuque street I've lived in since I was two years old. I go to school, when it's not summer like now. My life is pretty simple and consists of playing ball with my little brothers Jabaree and Kwasi, and riding bikes with my friends. You see, an ordinary person, really nothin' special. At least I used to think so. It wasn't my idea to change; the whole thing took me completely by surprise. One minute I'm like everybody else, the next moment someone decides to blink and it's all changed. Forever.

It was a sunny day in June a couple of days after school was out. My friends and I were all playing hide and seek. There weren't a lot of us, just Roberta, Paula and Paul (the twins) and me. I was it, as usual.

I'm always it because I never find anyone. It's not that I can't find them. To be exact, it's because I can. Confused?

I'll explain, I always know exactly where they are hiding. It's almost as if someone was watching them hide and then they come and whisper it to me. I feel this gives me an unfair advantage so I try really hard not to find them. Got it? Never mind. Like I said, we were playing hide and seek. And, I was just about to walk past Roberta, hiding in Mrs. Gutierrez's azalea bush for the third time, when Jamal walked by me. Jamal Lewis. Excuse me, The Jamal Lewis, captain of the football team at Jefferson Junior High and starting quarterback, tallest boy in school with kind gentle manners and the most delicious chocolaty-brown skin I had ever seen.

"Isn't that Jamal Lewis?" Roberta asked.

I was caught; maybe she hadn't seen me staring holes through that guy's body.

"Who?" I said trying to sound vague and distracted which I really was, actually. I was remembering the first time I'd ever seen him. I was running to gym class, because as usual I was going to be late. My head was down and I was trying to come up with a good excuse. As I rounded the corner, the building came into sight or, at least it would have if I'd been paying attention. Suddenly, I heard the scuff of feet and a shocked squeal as I kind of ran into Jamal. All right, I didn't kind of run into him; I plowed into him with enough force to send him and his adoring admirers flying. I didn't say anything. I was so embarrassed that I grabbed my stuff and took off. I'd been avoiding him ever since.

Roberta brought me back to the present by applying her elbow to the tender spot over my ribs.

"Ow! You mean Jamal from school." She didn't buy it for a moment. We'd known each other too many years for that. Our mothers were best friends, they had met in college. Her mom's degree was in social work and my mom's in criminal justice. Both wanted to return to the place where they'd grown up to make a difference in the community. It was purely accidental that they found themselves in the same building, so we grew up together. We went to the same day care centers and schools, and celebrated Christmas in her house and Kwanzaa in mine. Roberta let me off this time with only a frown and a quick flick of her braid, that coincidentally snapped the end of my nose (coincidence my eye!). To avoid another flick, I said, "Wonder what he's doing in this neighborhood? He lives near Buddy Todd Park."

"He's probably visiting David," said a high squeaky voice behind us. We turned to see who had spoken. Our eyes lighted on Paul and Paula, the twins. I'm not sure which one had spoken, because their voices have the same high nasal quality. Besides they hadn't been talking to us anyway. As usual they were talking to each other.

The two red heads were close together. It always shocks people at how much alike these two were. From hair color to hair cut, facial features, voices, likes and dislikes they mirrored each other in every way. Well, almost every way, since one is a boy and the other a girl.

"Paula,.. Paul,..!" It can be hard to get their attention when they're talking to each other, so I tried again only louder.

"Paula,.. Paul..!" They blinked sleepily, as if waking from a trance. Two pairs of hazel eyes looked toward us.

"Oh," they said at the same time in the same voice.

"Stop that, you know I hate it when you do that." Not very tolerant am I? Don't worry you'll get used to it, everybody does.

They smirked knowingly at each other. You know, sometimes I get the feeling that those two monsters do that on purpose just to see me lose control.

Roberta grabbed my arm as if to remind me of the last time I lost it, control that is. It had been nothin' nice.

"What did you say?" My smile was back in place and with full effect. I caught them off guard. Smiling in return, they were startled into answering my question.

"Jamal is probably going to talk to David, his best friend, about whatever has been bothering him."

"And how did you come to this conclusion?" You know I had to ask. Although looking back on it now, it probably wasn't a good idea. Because what followed next was a confusing mess of words like empirical, and the coefficient of the radical ratio, or some crazy madness similar to that. During this incredibly long explanation, Roberta and I stared at each other until we realized that our mouths were hanging open. Sometimes those twins really amaze me. Here we thought they spent all their time tinkering with their computers. Now, we find that they've come across a mystery, a mystery that is actually of interest to us. The worst part about the whole thing is that neither Roberta nor I had heard anything.

Rolling my eyes to heaven, I asked to be forgiven because I still wanted to choke those two until they passed out or turned blue, whichever came first. I made the mistake of looking over at Roberta.

She opened her eyes really wide, so that I could clearly see all the white surrounding her dark brown irises, then she started to grin. We both burst out laughing. Everything was okay again, it even had the added benefit of stopping the twins lecture on gathering data that had progressed to the point of formula drawing on the sidewalk with a discarded crayon. Roberta. What a friend.

"Okay, people, we all want to know what's going on. So, let's pool our info." A huddle was formed around the crayon markings on the sidewalk. Then, once we'd convinced the twins that we were sufficiently impressed with their formulae this is what came out:

Jamal Lewis
Age: 14
Residence: Two-story house across from Buddy Todd Park
Accomplishments: Captain both football and debate team, talented artist
Most important: NO GIRLFRIEND!! NO GIRLFRIEND!!

Unfortunately, none of this stuff, although very interesting, moved us any closer to knowing what was bothering this very accomplished, extremely fine young man.

I ended the meeting soon after the twins suggested hacking into the school's computer. They supposed that finding out his IQ would be of use because often IQ has a great deal to do with personality disorders. That's when I ended it. After all, even chronically nosy people have to draw the line somewhere.

Chapter 2

"Jamal, if you won't tell me what's wrong, I'm going to read my book." Jamal stared at David, from the window sill where he was sitting. He didn't feel like talking and there was no way he was going to try and cross the pit that was his friend's room to give him the pop in the mouth he so obviously needed.

The lump on the bed moved and stretched, dissolving into a long arm. The arm reached down and picked a book from the many piled high all over the floor.

"Okay, okay! I just didn't know how to begin and I really still don't." Jamal sighed deeply and turned back to the window. That strange girl was still out there, she and her friend with the long black braid. They were sitting on the steps of their apartment building, and appeared to be deep in conversation their heads close together. Suddenly, they stopped talking, and the strange one looked up. Straight at David's window.

If he hadn't know better, he would have thought that she knew he'd been thinking about her and that she could see not only him from that distance, but also his soul.

Without thinking about how it would sound he said, "She's looking at me."

"You mean Keisha. Oh, ignore it, she does that all the time." Jamal turned from the window to once again stare at his friend. David was still sometimes a mystery to Jamal. They'd become friends in the fifth grade, when he'd caught David reading in the bathroom. No, not Playboy, a mystery novel. Jamal could never understand why David didn't want anyone to know he loved to read. It was confusing, but it had never affected their friendship in a bad way. Besides, Jamal loved books too and had decided to overlook David's strangeness.

"What?" David looked up from his book to stare through the lenses of his precious glasses. Blue eyes, sandy blonde hair and the classical looks that girls all over town dreamed about. Most guys envied him his good looks. So, to make up for it, people liked to assume that he was stupid, or at least not very quick. They were wrong.

"Look, Lewis, forget about that girl. What's wrong WITH YOU?" Jamal tried to stall one last time, "What do you mean?"

David raised himself from his pillows and began to scratch at imaginary hair and beard, "Hum, let's see. We haven't worked on the crystal set for over two weeks. You walked around school like a zombie. Now, school's out for a couple of days and this is the first time I've seen or heard from you. Lastly, you're sitting over there staring out that stupid window trying to pretend that nothin' is wrong, when you're about to burst out cryin'. I'm not sure, but I'd be willing to bet, that even if I don't have enough evidence to convict, I could probably indict." (David always talked like the detectives in the novels to which he was addicted.)

The book he was holding suddenly flew across the room, nearly taking a piece out of one of Jamal's ears. He was used to it, Dave used books for punctuation.

"All right, that's it!! Tell me what's wrong or shed blood." Fitting actions to words, he stood, as best he could in the middle of all his books, and put up his fists. Considering that Jamal was twenty pounds heavier and at least a foot taller, David was crazy but there was no doubt that he was serious.

Jamal quickly raised his hands in defeat, "I'll tell you, just sit down man!" Taking a deep breath he let it all out in a rush of words.

"Something's wrong with my Mom and Pop."

"What do you mean something's wrong? They ignoring you, fighting each other, kicked you dog, what?!"

Jamal shook his head in frustration and tried again, "No, nothing like that, I can't explain. It's like I went to sleep and in the middle of the night somebody came into my house and took my parents away, or messed mine up so bad that they're unrecognizable. I don't know what to do, man. Just don't know what to do."

The fear and pain were woven all through Jamal's words and struck David's heart, and his eyes filled with tears in response.

"Ah, I'm sorry man. It's going to be okay," David said, trying to comfort Jamal; he roughly patted his friend's shoulder.

"You've come to the right place." He waited for Jamal to look up and meet his eyes, "together we can fix anything."

Four hours later, they decided they needed help. Actually David decided, right after Jamal lifted him off the floor by his neck.

"Dang," Jamal groaned from a pile of books on the floor, "what am I going to do?"

They'd switched places, with Jamal closer to the bed and David standing staring out of the window.

It was his turn to look out across the nearly-empty street. Paper blew from one gutter to the next. Suddenly, the moon, once hidden behind a large dark cloud, shone down onto a window, the window that was diagonal to his own-Keisha's window.

In a flash he knew how to help his friend. It wasn't going to be easy convincing either of them to fall in with his plan. But of the two, Jamal would probably be the hardest to convince. He wasn't going to worry about Keisha. When it came time to apply pressure, he had an ace in the hole.

Turning away from the window, he stumbled toward his friend and patted his shoulder. Jamal looked up, and David startled his friend with a beatific smile.

"Trust me."

Chapter 3

Later that same night, I Keisha Johnson who usually falls asleep instantly, find myself watching the full moon posing outside my window. The breeze, blowing my curtains, came from off the ocean miles away and was Santa Anna warm and scented by the Oleander growing in Mrs. Gutierrez's backyard.

Birds were singing their babies to sleep, and I still remember being envious of those baby birds. My mom had duty that night at the police station, and wouldn't be home until very early in the morning. I needed to get to sleep, but every time I closed my eyes I could see the worry on Jamal's face and I would be startled awake.

"What?" I asked myself for the hundredth time. Yes, I do talk to myself, and then I waited quietly for and answer. I know it sounds strange, but it works. Well, most of the time anyway. This time. Nothin'.

What could help me get to sleep? I tried it all, slugging my pillow or rolling over and giving my bear Frisco a good squeeze. (Don't you dare laugh.) Finally, I went for the one thing that is usually a guarantee when it comes to putting me to sleep. My science book. Just the thought of it was enough to cause my eyes to begin to roll to the back of my head. Unfortunately, the book was on the other side of the room in the roll top desk my grandfather had left me.

There was no need to turn on any lights because my shades were open, as they most always are, to let in the light from the street lamps outside my window. Okay, so maybe I'm still a little bit uncomfortable in complete darkness. This doesn't mean that I am afraid of the dark.

Oh, where was I? Yeah, on my way to my desk. When, suddenly, there was a sound against my window. A very loud sound. But small, none the less. Kinda like a "ping". I turned to stare, hoping to find the answer written in bold italicized letters on the pane.

It didn't come again, so I shrugged it off as a chocolate-chip-induced hallucination and went on my way. Suddenly, my window was assaulted by so many pings that I thought it was some kid who'd borrowed his dad's Uzi to write his name on the wall of my bedroom. Well, it could happen?!

I checked, from underneath my bed, to see if my window was still intact, or in pieces all over my floor. It was whole, but incredibly dirty.

Okay, if it wasn't a love-crazed, uzi-packin' teenager, who was it? Cautiously, I approached the window and slowly peered over the sill. You won't believe who was standing there. Jamal Lewis. Oh, yeah, David was there, too. Maybe opening the window without getting their attention first wasn't a good idea. I suppose it could also be argued that sticking my head out immediately wasn't either. Don't worry, I learned my lesson. It's surprising what a mouth full of dirt can do to improve one's reasoning abilities.

David started laughing, and Jamal just stood there doing a good imitation of a fly catcher.

"What..Do..You..Want."

David and Jamal exchanged looks. Whatever passed between them designated David as spokesperson.

"We need to talk to you."

"Do you realize what time it is?" Man, did that ever sound like something my mom would have said to me.

Silence reigned as I stared down onto two bowed heads. Neither head moved or said anything.

"If you don't have anything to say, I can assume you're just here to bug me," I paused, waiting for a response.

"I'm going back to bed." As I started to turn away, I was stopped by a soft brown voice.

"Wait," was all he said. It was enough. He had my undivided attention. Why did he have to speak? I could handle David, but Jamal was different. Something in the way he said that single word struck a cord with in me. I was going to get some answers. Don't ask me how I knew, I just did. Don't worry, you'll get used to it.

Jamal continued, "I know this is strange, but we just need to talk to you for five minutes, just five minutes." Man, was he fine.

No, that wasn't the only reason I was listening. It helped of course, but my special senses were going crazy. So you see the decision was out of my hands. You can see that, can't you?

Anyway.

All right, five minutes, but this had better be good." The guys slapped some dap and I turned to jump into my house shoes, pull on a long shirt over my pj's and a robe over the lot.

I quickly crossed the room and eased open my door. Staying low to the ground, I did my imitation of a cop entering a dangerous situation. I stuck my head into the hall and swiftly pulled it back inside long enough to see everything in the hall, but fast enough not to be seen myself. "Ow!" Police and detectives on T.V. never seem to whack themselves in the head. At least, I didn't scream.

Clutching my head and mouth, I eased the rest of my body through the door. The hallway past Ma's and Pop's room never seemed so long. Floor boards moaned and creaked under my tiptoeing feet. I passed the room where my Pop slept noisily, and one of the floor boars gave a loud rifle-like pow. This pow as luck would have it, happened at the same time Pop took a break from his breathing exercises with his nasal passages. The house went still.

"Keisha?"

My heart dropped into my toes. "Huh, pop?" That was me trying to sound out of it and sleepy.

"Girl, what are doing out there?"

"Bathroom." It wasn't quite a lie. I would go before I left the house.

"Oh," and the sawing within seconds was on once again.

Wiping not so imaginary sweat from my face, I quickly went to the bathroom, besides, if I hadn't had to before I certainly needed to now, and not just to keep from lying to my Dad.

The living room and front door presented no problem. I was outta there. Outside the sky clear and bright. Stars winked at me from a bed of deepest blue velvet. Pausing a moment to take some deep breaths, I thought about how much I love living on this street and in this neighborhood.

David and Jamal met me on my way down the stairs. Without a word, I pushed past them and continued to the bottom, where I turned right and rapped quietly at Roberta's window.

A few minutes more and a little more tapping, the curtain twitched open and a grumpy face looked out at me. Before opening her window, Roberta brushed her bans out of her face and checked over her shoulder to make sure I hadn't disturbed her little sister.

"Girl, this had better be good!" Did I mention that Roberta without eight to ten hours of sleep is not someone with whom you have conversation? Well, most people anyway.

I jumped right in, "Jamal and David are here!" I whispered loudly. That opened her eyes real quick.

"What up?"

"They want to talk to me about something."

"Can't it wait till the morning?"

"Evidently not, or I wouldn't be here." I'm not necessarily at my best without all that much sleep myself. I started again. "Besides, they seem prepared to throw rock's at my window till they break it."

The look she gave me was very hard.

"Goodnight!" She started to close the window.

Do you know, for an instant I thought about letting Roberta off the hook. After all, they hadn't asked to talk to her, and actually I didn't have to go with them myself. Dad was home and I could either wake him up or let them break my window which would wake him up. Or, they might eventually just go away because of frustration. All of these deep thoughts took only long enough to pull poor sweet little Roberta through her bedroom window by her braid.

I ignored all the words I was sure her mother would never believe her gentle daughter capable of using. I told her so, which caused her to talk faster and louder with much shaking of fingers in my face and head movements. The only thing that stopped her was seeing the guys smiling at her. Suddenly the Spanish tirade dried up like the desert, like I knew it would. After all, unlike me Roberta was better at pretending to be a very proper young lady, at least in public.

The wind picked up a bit and blew Ro's nightgown around. Then, it occurred to me that we were standing in clear view of any adult who might happen to look out a window and have a desire to disturb sleeping parents, mainly mine.

"Okay, where should we go?" Three blank faces looked back at me. I tried again.

"We can't stay here, someone could see us and then we're all busted." The fog in their eye's cleared and David and Jamal seemed at a loss. Not Ro. she looked over at me and we both began to grin. David and Jamal looked at the two of us standing there smiling, then at each other.

Clueless.

Finally they couldn't stand it any longer, and had to ask what was so funny. Of course, we couldn't tell them the truth or they would have thought we were crazy. The truth is that sometimes, when conditions are right, our minds move as one and we think the same thoughts at the same time as smoothly and beautifully as two people sharing one mind and body. We couldn't have explained, and besides we had no intention to do so even if we could, se we said simply, "The Tower" in one voice with the exact same inflection and tone. Who says the twins have a monopoly on being irritating.

Chapter 4

Meanwhile across town in the Del Rio industrial park.--

The wheeze pop of bald light bulbs fill a small section of the massive structure with sharp yellow light. Bulbs strung loosely on 20-foot wires hung in a rectangular arrangement from the ceiling created an island amidst the gloom for the two figures working drearily on and on. Light bounced around the table where they were busily taking readings and measurements. Mrs. Dr. Lewis reached across what seemed to be a mile of white table and glass to grab the hand her husband was holding out to her. Both sets of strong African features were pinched and drawn with tiredness. Brown eyes met long enough to communicate their mutual fear and desperation. For a moment, they really were on an island but not this cold, fear-filled one. No, the tropical island where they had met twenty years before. A little cove where they had swam, fallen in love and planned their life together. This was a memory that had carried them through many difficult situations, but it wasn't to be allowed this time.

From overhead, a booming voice interrupted the quiet moment.

"How very touching, and while I'm sure many might find your little display tender and moving, it just makes me want to vomit!"

NOW BACK TO WORK!!

The scientists squeezed fingers gently and pulled slowly away to follow orders. They'd learned fairly early on that disobedience only separated them. Turning, they continue down opposite sides of the table, both their thoughts went to Jamal.

High above in the control booth, a small whinny voice broke the relative silence of the room.

"I believe, Sir, that you're going to have a problem with those two." The man who spoke was medium height and weight, brown hair and eyes. He was also very pale; not the California pale of someone who had a tan but has lost it. No, more the cave dweller pale, as if this poor man rarely, if ever, saw the outdoors. The speaker had a lean face, that was void of any expression, except subservience as he stared fixedly at the tall figure who stood before the mounted monitors along the walls. This man who commanded all of the others attention, would have been swallowed by darkness if not for the illumination of the miniature T.V. screens.

The man turned toward his servant. Yes, servant, for that was what the little brown man was to this person. This person with cold white eyes that seemed to bore into the little man's suddenly-trembling body. No words were spoken, and Wendal, the little brown man, began to regret ever having said anything. Quickly, he remembered all the people who had caught his master's attention. Whether positively or negatively, it didn't matter, the result was always the same.

Those eyes that could pierce the strongest soul, suddenly lit with glee which in no way diminished Wendal's fear. Sometimes, his master was most dangerous when happy. A melodious chuckle escaped pale lifeless lips and, "Oh dear me, I certainly hope that you are once again incorrect."

With a very small, yet elegant flick of his hand, he removed an imagined speck of dust from the blazing white jacket cuff and turned back to the view screens. The poor man behind him took advantage of this chance to mop his forehead and attempt to still the shakes running up and sown his spine.

A match flared, shining harshly on the soulless white eyes, paper-pale face, and hair so blonde it appeared translucent in the match light. Ever so slightly, the master squinted at the large window directly in front of him where he could watch Wendal twitch. Inhaling, he blew smoke at his reflection.

"Yes indeed, for their sake, I hope your wrong." While in the distance, two forms moved blurrily about their duties. Isolated by the warm light that surrounded their little island, they prayed silently for a miracle. For although neither of them spoke the words, they both understood that their lives didn't mean anything to the people who held them.

Chapter 5

The squeak of bike chains and the distant sound of traffic on Mission Boulevard filled the night air. Moon glow was the only light to be seen on Roosevelt Street that night. And being full, it was more than sufficient for our needs. I was followed closely, first by Roberta, then the guys in some kind of order I'm sure. Roosevelt was the road that went through our neighborhood, then raced all the way through Oceanside, curving and dipping and rising until it nearly touched the ocean as it met the Strand. That road is really a bike rider's dream, and on a night like that it added an extra edge to the adventure we had set for ourselves.

We crossed the railroad tracks that were the last marker prior to the long dip that sent us tumbling toward the Strand, the beach and ultimately (if conditions were really good) the ocean. Roberta and I took the hill at top speed. I leaned to the right, shot around the corner like a bullet. My braids whipped around my head, the feeling was incredible I laughed from the sheer joy of it. Roberta echoed my laughter, but the boys were as silent as stone. Boys are so strange.

Roberta moved up to my left side and we raced until the road began to curve away from the beach. Brakes squealed and rubber burned as we stopped together. We turned and watched the boys make their way to the sand. "What's their problem?" Ro. whispered in my ear. I just shrugged my shoulders, marveling at the way she says the words I think.

"I don't know, man, but something is definitely going on with those two." Roberta moved closer to me as the guys walked their bikes toward us. Jamal's face was set so hard you could almost feel the anger coming from him, David was talking real fast and grabbing his arm every few steps to get his attention. Whatever he said must have worked, because he stopped shaking his head and appeared to actually be listening.

David, the spokesman, cleared his throat when they reached us. I suppose it was his way of bringing us back to the problem at hand. I blinked and waved my hand in a vague sort of way, gesturing toward a clump of bushes and grass near the apartment building that marked the end of the public beach.

It was their turn to once again look at us as if we were crazy. We turned away and moved in the direction we wanted them to go, and directed them to follow us.

After about 50 feet, we stopped in front of a door, well-hidden within the bushes. It was my turn to be look out, so I stood back to back with Roberta and checked the beach while Ro. knocked loudly at the door. After listening for a small space of time, we went in.

The musty smell of seldomly stirred up dust and old rotting wood met us at the door. Ah, the glorious smells of home. This place used to be the top of an abandoned lifeguard tower. Missing tower #6, to be exact. They had intended to haul the little room away to the dump. Somehow though, when the flat-bed truck came it had mysteriously vanished. Actually there was nothing mysterious about it; a group of us kids had begun to play in and around the tower.

Before it came down, about twenty of us met secretly and decided to make the tower go away. So, one night a hole was dug and Lifeguard Station 6 was half buried. The workmen hadn't really wanted to move it anyway so they really didn't look too hard when they couldn't find it that next morning. Everyone else quickly lost interest after the first few shovel - fulls of dirt had been thrown. So, now it belongs to just Roberta and me.

Roberta walked to the wall directly across from the door and lifted the kerosene lantern from under the lone crate, where we kept it for our late night adventures. Okay, so this was the first time we'd had a chance to use it. Girl Scouts are always prepared.

Quickly, we lit the lantern and arranged ourselves almost accidentally by gender. Roberta took over the crate near the lamp while I tried to hide in a dark corner on a small rug we'd scavenged from a dumpster.

"Have a seat." Roberta was playing hostess, which was fine with me. There was to much going on inside for me to be able to handle the amenities that entertaining company required.

David took the only seat that was really a chair, and Jamal choose to stand.

Then, there was silence. Silence except for the sound of waves brushing the sand and the squeak of the mouse we fed whenever we visited our little house.

No one wanted to begin so Ro. did. "Now guys, you went to a lot of trouble to get us here," she looked quickly over at me. I had nothing to say so she continued, "What's so important that it couldn't wait until tomorrow?"

David and Jamal both kind of looked uncomfortable at that. I was glad she had started that way, I didn't understand at the time, but I wanted this to be anything but easy for these two. Especially David. No particular reason really, I just have a mean streak sometimes.

"We've got a problem," from spokesman David.

"Why are you telling us? Why not the police, or your parents. I mean don't you have any friends besides each other?" Did I mention that Roberta hates to be awakened?

She started some lovely fireworks though. David began to turn red from the tips of his ears down. He kind of looked the way I'm sure a tea kettle must feel, so I waited. He exploded. He yelled at Roberta and she yelled right back at him, but in Spanish of course. Wow, what a volatile scene that was. I moved toward Ro. intent on bringing her back to the present. Jamal beat me to the punch.

"Stop!" not really a yell - just said forcefully. It got everyone's attention, and we all returned to our seats quickly and quietly just as if the principal had stepped into a rowdy class room. Now, normally, I would have reacted differently. You know, woman of the Nineties and all that. Something about the way Jamal started pacing caused me to sit back and wait. He went back and forth, back and forth. None of us were willing to break the silence or stop him from his trance-like pacing. We could almost see the words being drawn from the air around him. He was gathering his dignity and strength and shrugged into it like a protective covering.

I was studying the floor, waiting for that next shoe to hit the floor. When I saw one of Jamal's shoes that is, he'd finally come to a stop directly in front of me. Looking up to meet his eyes took quite a while and what I found there made the breath catch in my throat.

Grandma said that the soul resides in the eyes, and the soul peering at me spoke of the heartbreak he was experiencing. Deep down I knew I was in trouble and I began to pray.

"Look, I know this is strange," he began "and to be honest I don't know why we're here either." He looked over at David who put his hands up defensively. Jamal shook his head and turned back to me with a sigh, he continued to explain.

"About two weeks ago, my Mom and Dad started getting these really strange phone calls. At the beginning I would answer the phone and it would be this extremely polite English guy. Whichever of my parents who took the call wouldn't talk for very long and they'd hang up angry or afraid. Finally, two days ago, I answered the phone and again it was the same English guy, but this time he wasn't in a good mood. He wasn't polite either. We'd been in the kitchen. Mom and Dad were finishing up the paper work from the day's experiments and talking over their findings. I guess I made a sound or they saw the look on my face, whatever, but my Dad took the phone. I went back to the table and tried to be quiet so they'd forget I was in the room. There wasn't anything to hear. Dad just kept saying no, over and over. This went on for a while until Dad's eyes turned really angry and he slammed the receiver down and turned off the ringer. They wouldn't look at me or at each other. I asked them about the call, and they lied."

Questions were racing around in my head but only two seemed to make sense, so I asked those. "They have lied to you before, right? And, what makes you so sure they weren't tellin' you the absolute truth?" The room felt empty of everyone but Jamal and me. Really just me and the mystery unfolding around me. Everyone else just sort of faded into the background, including "Mr. Fine" himself.

"My parents have never lied to me." The disbelief on our faces must have been comical, because he said with irritation, "Never, until the day before yesterday. Now, as for how I knew, that I just can't explain. I just did." He finished and

I found myself wanting to run, I didn't want him to say anything else so I could just disappear.

He didn't stop, "This morning I woke up and my Mom was making breakfast and Dad was reading the paper and smoking a pipe." He said it like they'd been baking kittens in pie crust.

"Okay, they're boring but what's the big deal." I was confused but still sure the shoe was hanging by a lace.

"No! My parents don't eat breakfast. They mix a protein drink in their lab. If I want bacon and eggs, I have to make them myself. More than breakfast were the other things." I was surprised to see him hesitate. "They were dressed really weird. My mom was wearin' a white apron and her hair was in a bob." He looked at our blank faces and explained. "My Mom's hair has been in dred lochs since before I was born. Her hair is long and kinky. She says it's the original hair and nothing short of death would make her remove them. That's it, I know it's hard to believe but my parents are gone. I don't know where they've gone or who took them, but I want them back!"

Back was said in a near shout that probably startled Jamal as much as any of us. Uncomfortably, we shifted around in our seats and Jamal turned with his back toward us.

I began to shrink inside again. It was time. In my life, destiny steps in all the time and snatches me into bad situations. The box was getting smaller, and the running space was almost gone. I got desperate and I looked to Roberta for help. She'd been watching me for some sort of sign, and I guess what she saw wasn't exactly what she'd hoped for. But, Ro.'s tough. With or without me, she was in it for all that she was worth.

"All right, maybe I missed it, but exactly what does that have to do with Keisha and me?"

David was quick to jump in, "Actually, we don't need you for anything. We need Keisha to help us find out what's going on."

"Keisha!" her voice rose at least two octaves, her face flushed and she came to her feet ready to do battle. "The last I heard O.P.D. was still located on Mission Avenue not on Dubuque Street. I do understand your confusion. There are two Johnsons in that apartment building that are indeed police officers. You just picked the wrong one."

David took a step forward. From his words, that step was more than physical. "Look you might as well sit down because Keisha is going to help us, which means that you'll be helping us too."

Now why did he have to say that?

The next thing you know that braid was over Ro.'s shoulder. If I hadn't jumped in at that moment, once again it would have been on. First I tried to reason with them, "Wait, wait," it didn't work. They just stood nose to nose glaring into each others eyes. They couldn't hear me.

"What makes you think we can help?" I was speaking to Jamal, who'd turned in surprise to watch the fight about to begin. "Don't look at me, it was his idea," pointing toward his foolish friend who was still locked in a battle of wills with my foolish friend.

Pushing my chair back caused a huge wave of dust to rise from the floor. I stepped between the two combatants and pushed my level-headed pal into her chair.

We exchanged places, and I found myself looking ever so slightly down on David while Ro. had faced him head on. Yeah, I know it's silly but those two inches gave me the advantage, and he knew it. Before I could take control of the situation, a strange gleam appeared in David's eye and he took a seat and crossed his legs. In a most irritating way, I might add. Here it comes. I thought to myself. I wasn't ready.

"I'm just wasting my breath trying to appeal to the sensitive side of girls like you," he paused to look at both of us with a nearly mystical grin, "Ain't I?"

Roberta was bristling at the word "girl". You see, we were young women, and if our maturity wasn't enough to convince you of that fact, we were more than willing to beat the ever lovin' crap out of whoever doubted it. I gave her the look and she settled down and crossed her arms over her chest. Turning back to David, I wasn't really surprised to find my arms crossed over mine as well. It is my defensive, yet comfort, posture. I knew eventually I was going to need all the comfort I could possibly get.

He continued, "Since you want to play this ugly, I can be ugly."

"You know that's right." from Roberta leaning against the wall. He ignored her, all his attention was for me. All I could do was wait.

He kind of chuckled at the look on my face. A desperate little sound, not really a laugh, filled with the frustration that only a friend could feel for the pain of another.

I was weakening and that child hadn't even opened his mouth. "You're going to help us. Not because you want to, but because if you don't, I'm going to tell the school, the neighborhood and anyone else I can get to listen what kind of freak you are." I wasn't surprised. Ro's gasp told me she was. I felt a bit of a grin sneak its way across my face. If that little bit shocked her, she'd better take a tighter grip on her shorts because she hadn't heard nothin' yet.

David rolled his eyes toward heaven and took the step that would change everyone in that room in ways that none of us could have ever imagined. And although I knew I had no choice, I wouldn't let it be easy for him. I could feel the words forming inside his head.

Matching his chuckle of minutes before, I made a last attempt to keep us from tumbling over the edge. "Freak?" Ice dripped from every letter, Grandma would have been proud. You see, Grandma was filled with power. She was believed to have caused the snow storm of "69" when someone accused her of spreading gossip. Sorry, that's another story.

Where was I? Oh, I remember.

"Freak, nobody is going to believe that. I've never had a boyfriend and the only boys I talk to besides Paul are my brothers Jabaree and Kwasi." Behind me Roberta laughed so hard she fell off her chair.

David's face began to change colors from tan to paper white to pink, then red and slightly purple just around his ears. For a second, I thought he was going to go up in flames like a Roman candle. Relief covered me like a blanket.

No. It hadn't been what I had expected, and we were out of there. I grabbed Roberta and pushed her toward the door. Our feet made small scuffing noises on the packed sand floor. Small puffs of dirt rose up to meet us as we pushed open the door. Behind us, Jamal quietly began to cuss, whether at David or at himself I didn't know. I suspect neither did he. I didn't stop to find out; I just kept pushing Roberta out into the warm ocean breeze, hoping I could get away before David regained his momentum.

The wind had picked up while we'd been inside and the waves were tall and churning, bearing the news of an approaching storm. There was an electrical charge in the air stopping me in my tracks while the wind played in the braids around my head. The elements were aligned against me. There was nowhere to run. Behind me the door burst open and I felt David come to a halt. Before he could speak, I turned toward him. The resignation on my face made him hesitate. He persevered and took up where he'd left off in the "tower".

"That's not the kind of Freak I meant and you know it!" Roberta moved up behind me, quietly lending support I hadn't even known I needed.

Dessie D. Moore

Isn't she great!

Jamal was outside now and had taken the same position behind David. The look he sent me spoke more of uncertainty than of challenge. David lent closer and spoke almost in a whisper that the other two had to strain to hear. To me it sounded as loud as a whisper during silent prayer at church. "I watch you," my breathing slowed and suddenly peace found me at last. He seemed to expect me to say something. But I was listening to the wind and the roar of the ocean. The voices were getting louder.

"I've seen you talking to people who weren't there, and to animals. I've seen you come outside and pull some kid out of a quiet street minutes before a car zoomed through the place he or she had been." He paused to breath. "Before you say "coincidence" I've seen one other thing." I'd begun to smile both inside and out. I'd underestimated this pretty boy jock. Even though I had some of his secrets as well as he had mine. The purity of my smile confused him. He continued, "I've seen you move things when you think no one is looking, like you curtains, rocks and many other things, but I wasn't sure. Not until two weeks ago, when you couldn't get to Javier in time to keep him from falling over the rail of your building." He looked at me in admiration. "You'd started to run but realized not you, nor anyone else, would make it in time. Everyone ran and screamed but you stopped. That's what made me pay closer attention."

My grin widened as I remembered that day. You see Javier is Roberta's baby brother. He's just two. The ice cream man had stopped his truck down the street from us. Javier had wanted an ice cream, and he had been visiting my mom while his Mom and Dad went to the store. Mom had to do something in another room and Javier climbed over the child security door. By the time anyone had noticed he had, he was trying to squeeze himself through the bars of the rail. All I could see were chubby little arms and legs waving between the bars. My feet took flight and I started yelling for my mom at the top of my lungs before anyone else had seen him. A split second later I realized mom couldn't hear me and none of us would reach him in time. I stopped, not caring that I might be caught, Javier was my chiquito amigo. Standing still, I gathered myself and found my circle of calm. The wind came to me-swiftly surrounding me, filling me. It wasn't much, what I did. Just a little push. Well, and of course there was the wall of wind I'd had to surround him with to keep him from going back into the same position from which I'd so recently removed him. It was the only thing that set him to crying, not being able to move. But, at least it kept him safe until Mom could come and soothe his tears. Afterward, I'd had to sit down on the ground and shed a few tears of my own. It was over quickly and I'd thought that my little bit of tampering had gone unnoticed. At least I'd hoped it had, but somehow deep down I'd known it hadn't. Now, here was the evidence that I was right.

Oh, well, you can't have everything.

David had concluded his tale while I'd been thinking about Javier. The look I was getting from the guys was both a mixture of admiration and a great deal of confusion. Roberta, on the other hand, was using her elbow trying to dig information out of my spine.

Quickly, I agreed to help. Not for the reasons that David had given. I wasn't afraid of these people and I knew, no matter what he'd said, David would never tell. He was desperate, but he knew enough about the way people treated you when you were different that he would never willingly drop a dime. Why did I agree? It's crazy, but the wind told me I must and the ocean instructed me to accept the destiny my inheritance required of me.

Our investigation would begin the next morning at nine o'clock in front of Jamal's house. The ride home was silent, and ended at the foot of my stairs where we split up. The guys went back to David's. They left, and Roberta told me quite clearly how she felt about my little deception. I thought she would go on all night, but somehow she finally realized that no matter what she said I wasn't ready to talk, so she gave up - for the moment and went inside her apartment.

I paused at the top of the stairs. The stars glowed down on me like the older sisters I'd begun to believe they were. My feelings about the next day were hard to describe. Anticipation, but not the good kind you feel right before diving into water you know is cold. No it was more like the night before an appointment at the dentists. You know, not necessarily something bad but with the dentist there is always that chance. Pale blue clouds rolled in from the ocean covering the already darker blue of the sky in patches.

Strangely, the clouds actually made the moon and the stars shine more brightly. The sky moved me to say my nightly prayers before going in, and for good measure I called the spirits of my ancestors and thanked them for their guidance. The house was quiet. No one had noticed my absence. After getting ready of bed, the second time, I was drawn once again to my window. Across the way, a figure stood staring back at me. Jamal, all I could see was a silhouette but I knew it was him. For a moment I couldn't stop myself feeling his feelings. Sadness. Worry. His parents. The four of us all mixed together.

Then suddenly his thoughts turned to me alone. Quickly, I blocked him from my mind and turned away.

I know. Why didn't I find out what he was thinking before I backed out. Tempting though it always was, Grandma Flora always said that people who eavesdrop usually hear things they would rather not have known.

Okay, okay. So that's not necessarily the only reason I don't listen in. Lets just say that experience is the best teacher. Nough said?

Where was I? Oh yeah.

I turned away from my window and climbed into bed. Head touched pillow and that's all she wrote.

Chapter 6

$\mathcal{T}$he house was what I had expected. Directly across from Buddy Todd Park, it was a two story with pretty curtains and yes, a white picket fence not meant to keep anyone out, just for decoration, the fence a frame for an already pretty picture. The lawn was well kept, well enough that I suspect someone came once a week with toe nail clippers and clipped each blade individually.

The four of us parked our bikes on the side of the house where a gate hid the family trash from the road. Since we'd set out just a little while before, silence had reigned from the moment Dubuque Street was left in the dust. Jamal took the lead, the key sounding loudly in the lock before he pushed open the door. With a brief hesitation, he stepped into the darkness beyond the porch and the rest of us followed suit.

The temperature outside was 80 degrees, but once inside we were chilled to the bone. We looked around, and found ourselves in what was obviously a living room. Nothing special about it really. Just a room definitely used by a family. (except for the wires all over the place that sent company heading our way) Couch and love seat braced two walls. A beat-up recliner shared leaning space with another couch. In the center of the room was a large mahogany coffee table draped in Mudd cloth and topped with African Tribal sculpture and magazines, with an added covering of about an inch thick of dust. The door was left open and some of those dust particles danced in the light.

To the right of the door hung a medium-sized gilded mirror immediately beneath which sat a small table with a tray that had to have been part of a set that came with the mirror. Unopened mail and a set of keys rested inside the mirrored bottom, as if someone had just come in and had tossed them there automatically.

Jamal crossed the floor and leaned against the staircase. We shuffled in one bye one, with David taking up the rear and closing the door after him.

We were finally here, after a sleepless night for all of us, and none of us knew where to start. Well, maybe not all of us? Okay, I knew where to start; I just didn't want the responsibility. They were already leaning heavily in my direction for leadership, and Lord knows I didn't want the job. I was pretty sure I couldn't afford the price that was going to be paid for whatever this was we were getting ourselves into. Regardless of how I felt, I'd really all ready had my chance to protect myself and I hadn't taken it. So I took charge.

"All right, we're here," looking at Jamal "So how many rooms do we need to search." Now, you know he paused before he answered.

"Well, on the first floor there's the formal living room." He pushed himself away from the staircase and pointed toward his left, drawing our eyes toward the large arch that led to a very fancy living room. Excuse me, a white living room. Roberta and I were mystified. You see, we're allergic to white anything. Nothing stayed white on or around the two of us for long.

"I'm not searching that room," I said to myself. Looking over at Ro. I could tell she was thinking the same thing.

"The family room is through there too," Jamal continued. Turning toward the right he gestured in that direction, "Through there is the kitchen, laundry room and stairs to the basement." Ro. mouthed basement at me with her eyes opened really wide. I shushed her and tried to ignore her in order to pay attention.

"Upstairs are our bedrooms and the office my parents use when they're writing reports or sending and receiving data."

"That's it?" More a statement than a question. Yeah, there was a little sarcasm in there too. I'm only 13, gimme a break. Jamal didn't hear the sarcasm because he answered my question.

"Oh, yeah, there's the attic."

David cleared his throat, "Okay, ladies, let's separate into teams. We can cover more ground that way." Considering how he was looking at Ro. I was sure he wasn't talking about girls on one team and boys on another. Ro. got the message too because her arms were crossed and he was getting her best blank look. Which didn't mean anything to him, but told me he didn't have a chance. Jamal was paying none of us any attention, he was staring at a picture of his family taken during happy times. I don't think he'd even heard us.

"No, dear," That was me. "We'll stay together." David tried to interrupt, but I stopped him with a wave of my hand. "Yes, I know. It will take longer, but if we stay together it's less likely that we'll miss anything."

He had nothing to say to that, so we started searching the first floor. We searched everywhere. And I do mean everywhere. Under the couches, under the fluffy pillows on the couches, behind pictures on the walls. We tapped the walls for hidden panels, David's idea. We also checked the refrigerator including the ice trays, Ro.'s idea. We lifted, pulled and took apart whatever we could lift or pull. Finishing up the first floor, we attacked the second. By unspoken and mutual consent we left the basement for last. In record time, we searched the second floor and the attic All we got for our trouble were faces full of cobwebs, a knock on Jamal's head and the joy of finding out how embarrassed he was to have Ro. and I going through his underwear drawer. Other than that, we had absolutely nothin' and I do mean nothin'!

In frustration, a break was called and we flopped on the staircase near the top, lost in our own thoughts. I can only guess at what anyone else might have been thinking, but I was listening to the voices. Voices from the past. I could hear the people who lived here. The Lewis's were all around me. I could feel their presence in every piece of furniture, paper or clothing they wore or touched. I was with them when the phone calls began. I didn't know who or what they were about. I just picked up emotional pictures. I tried to shut out the voices of this family - of theses people. I didn't want the others to know how this was affecting me. I'd caught the looks they'd all been shooting my way all morning. I knew they wanted to ask me about my skill, ability whatever you want to call it. As a matter of fact, Roberta was after me so hard for information earlier in the day we'd almost started fighting for the first time in years. The only thing that stopped what might have been a superior brawl was the boys riding up besides. I really didn't need them asking anymore questions.

A couple of groans and stretches and I was ready to tackle the last part of this house, so filled with happy loving memories that I felt like I was being attacked. Yes, it is as creepy feeling as it sounds. Lucky it's not you.

Ro. once again started the ball rolling in the correct direction. "Well, we can't sit here all day!" I stood and stretched and weaved my way through the legs and down the stairs. I turned to look back up when I reached the bottom. When I did, I slammed my nose dead in the center of Jamal's chest. I took a quick step back before I fell over either backwards or all over Jamal. He didn't look like he would have minded, but I certainly would. After all, I needed to concentrate. Both David and Ro. had silly grins on their faces when they joined us at the foot of the stairs. I frowned at Ro. and tried really hard not to look at Jamal at all.

As often is the case, Ro. saved my bacon (excuse the pork analogy) again. She grinned at Jamal who was staring at me, and said with a dramatic wave of her hand, "Your house, your show, lead the way."

With a last look, he brushed past and went around the staircase into the Arch that opened into the kitchen. It was a regular sort of kitchen, copper pots hanging over an island made of some kind of white substance. In fact, the whole kitchen was white and sterile looking. You know, like a hospital.

Jamal headed toward the back door, but before reaching it, he turned left. He stood facing another less visible door set flush with the wall. Jamal gave it a bit of a push and with a slight click, pressed the door, swinging it outward. Inside the door was an elaborately built-spice rack. It was well lit, a cubby not more than 5ft. long and slightly octagonal in shaped. Along the walls, sat sacks and barrels filled with rice and beans, grains and oats. Garlic and onions hung from the ceiling along with many drying herbs.

Jamal noticed our expressions of surprise, and he explained, "My Mom and Dad believe in eating whole foods and make most everything we eat from scratch whenever possible." He looked around and said almost to himself, "That's how I knew those people weren't my parents. Dad would have been helping cook, and they would never have given me that foul garbage to eat." For the first time he was angry, and I think it kind of scared him. He shook it off and walked to the far wall of the pantry. A large shelf covered with home preserves turned out to be another concealed door. I couldn't hold it in any longer, I had to ask.

"What's up with all these hidden doors? You said your parents were scientists, but this place has the atmosphere of a "007" movie. I mean is "Q" going to jump out and demonstrate on something?" He didn't take offense, he just grinned. "Well, you see it's like this. Sometimes my parents work for the Government." We stared at him in shock. "You know, the Governments always worries about national security so they installed ass of the hidden stuff as a kind of bonus."

That left me with nothing to say. It doesn't happen very often, so enjoy it.

The door opened at the top of a narrow stairway down which we followed Jamal. The only light we had to see by came from the open door and the room we just left. At the bottom, Jamal touched a lighter-colored panel on the wall. A hum began all over the room and florescent lights came on and ran the length, which of course was as long as the house. And I'd thought the kitchen looked like a hospital room. The floor was white linoleum. The walls were smooth and painted white. It looked so clean it made you feel that you could eat off the floor, no problem. Contraptions along the north wall would have made you hesitate to eat anywhere in this room, let alone on the floor.

Although the Doctors Lewis hadn't been down here for a couple of days, the test tubes and bowls and beakers of their trade, hissed and sang merrily though unattended. It was a hypnotic sort of thing, and I'd been standing watching it fizz and drip for a couple of minutes before I'd realized everyone else had already begun searching the room. The voices started up again, but this time it was with pictures. A phantom Mrs. Doctor Lewis brushed past me. She was intent on the papers in her hand. I looked around at the other guys. They were still searching busily. Of course, I was the only one losing it and seeing people who couldn't possibly be there. Oh, well, might as well go with the flow. I followed the phantom to the wall farthest from where anyone else was searching, the northeast corner of the room to be exact. She touched the bottom right corner of the portrait, and the picture rolled up into the inside of the frame. The phantom looked over her shoulder, toward me.

Yes, I know it's strange, but that's what happens sometimes. She winked and melted away. After my encounter, I walked toward the painting and stood gazing up at the father of the peanut, George Washington Carver, great African American scientist and inventor.

"Keisha girl, what are you looking at?' Ro walked over and stood beside me, while I gazed up at the painting like a zombie. We looked up at the painting of this cinnamon brown older gentleman who came before and made so many things possible for the rest of us.

Enough of the hero worship. I looked over at Ro. and once she looked back I gave her my most mysterious smile and pushed the funny spot on the corner of the painting just the way I'd seen Mrs. Doctor Lewis do moments before. Sure enough, the painting rolled up revealing a safe front.

"ALL RIGHT!" that was from David when he noticed us standing in front of the safe. It hadn't occurred to him that I hadn't actually been searching the room. Roberta and Jamal were another matter entirely. The two of them were trying to pierce holes through my head with their eyes.

I tried to divert attention from me to the flashing lights of the safe. "Uh, ha, ha. Yeah, what have we here?" A little square pad of numbers ranging from 0-9 and above the first row were two lights one red and one green. Our luck being what it was, the red light was on.

I looked to Jamal and said hopefully, "You do know the combination. Right?"

He smiled, "Oh yeah, I didn't know there was a safe there, but of course I know the combination the minute you found it."

He has a very smart mouth on him, doesn't he? Amazingly enough, I didn't mind, and smiled at him in return. Wow, did I already mention that his eyes were a most beautiful shade of brown? We stood there like two idiots smiling at each other, until David said something, I don't remember what, and started laughing. I looked away and felt the heat rising up into my face. Yet another reason to love my deep brown skin. Beautiful and also hides blushes. I looked at David and said in my quietest voice, just loud enough for him to hear, "read any good books lately?" Unfortunately David doesn't have my chocolaty brown skin. The flames rose from his neck to up past his ears and into his hair line. He started sputtering. Jamal smiled at me in rueful admiration and shook his head before turning David away to have a whispered conversation with him on the other side of the room.

Ro. gave me a quick elbow and a questioning look. I just shook my head "no" in return, not dismissing her question, just putting off until later. I put my arm over her shoulder and turned her toward the wall safe. "You know, man," I said to her, "This looks like a job for the twins." She smiled and we turned away to ask Jamal which phone we could use.

Chapter 7

(Back at the industrial park)

I n the control booth, Wendal busied himself with the housekeeping kind of jobs that drove most people quite insane. But you see, that sort of thing never bothered Wendal anymore because he was more than half - way insane anyway. Working for his master had done that to him. So, while his genius intellect was still intact, the rest of him had about as much will as a marshmallow. He dusted cleaned the mirrors so many times that the red flashing light was making beautiful patterns the entire length of the pane.

He stood lost in the glow of light for what had seemed like forever. The next thing he knew there was a presence standing next to him. He jumped about a foot both away and off the ground. When he landed he began to shake.

"Enjoying the lovely light are we?" Samuel moved closer to the panel of T.V. monitors and flicked a switch immediately beneath the small flashing red light bulb. A white pinpoint of light expanded and filled the screen with tiny figures in a well-lit white basement. It was impossible to tell exactly what the small people were doing but they were working industriously at whatever it was. Samuel turned from the monitor and strolled gently toward the cowering Wendal.

He ran his hand over Wendal's thinning crop of brown hair, down to his wet cheek and chin. He cupped the poor man's face and moved in close. Pale eyes scanned the face so near his own. And he was pleased by what he saw.

"Once again you have displeased me." But, he smiled, "Yet in the very midst of my displeasure, you give such wonderful fear response." He patted Wendal on the cheek and turned to pick up the flip phone. Wendal slowly stepped back into a dark corner. A strange gleam appeared in his eye, it was there and gone almost unnoticeable. Then again, so was Wendal.

"Yes, send a couple of the men over to the Lewis' residence." He turned to look out at the expanse of the warehouse below. "Make sure they understand that we need the computer disks and files, whatever there is. Oh, and tell them to grab the boy too."

He hung up the phone and started to do his favorite thing, remembering the fear and pain he'd inflicted on someone weaker than myself.

Chapter 8

Paul and Paula had arrived about ten minutes before, and had shoved us to the other side of the room. What did they have to do that for? David, Jamal, Roberta and I, we all sat together watching the twins try to crack the safe. They were in their element, but the four of us had nothing to say. You know how it is. You get all caught up in something, then suddenly you're not doing anything, and you feel useless and kind of stupid. Well, that's how I'm sure the three of them were feeling.

Jamal started staring at me. You know the way. It was kind of cool, so I did my job as a woman of the 90's. "What are you looking at?" That's right. I got defensive! You want to make something of it? "Do you know what that silly guy did?" He started grinnin'. And suddenly Roberta and David found things elsewhere that required their attention and nearly broke their necks trying to get to them.

Roberta and I had been sitting on one of those chairs with wheels. The guys were sitting on the floor, since we had the chairs. My traitor of a friend had taken off at the same time as the wanna-be sleuth, David. Jamal moved himself gracefully along the floor. Where he stopped directly in front of me, staring up at me. You know, usually looking down on someone gives you at least a feeling of having the upper hand. Yet there I was sweating in shorts and a tank top. And he just sat there, looking up at me, close enough to touch if I had half-a-mind to. I smiled, don't know why. I just felt it rise up inside of me and splatter itself across my face. His smile, on the other hand, was gone, only to be seen in his eyes. It was a perfect moment. A moment that makes my breath catch in my throat. Even now. Neither of us said anything. We just sat there letting our eyes become accustomed to the sight of one another.

"Okay, guys, it's almost ready." We looked away and toward where the voice had come from. Paul was smiling at us and waving us toward the safe where Paula was attaching wires from her notebook computer to spaces on the face of it. We gathered around the pair of them and watched while Paula pressed many keys rapidly until she was satisfied with the outcome. Jamal and I worked really hard at pretending that we didn't notice each other.

Although standing pretty close, we made absolutely sure we didn't touch, even accidentally.

Paula brushed her fiery red hair away from her sweaty forehead. "Here we go." She said with a grin over her shoulder before she firmly placed a bony finger on the return key.

Her computer went crazy. Lights flashed and numbers scrolled down the screen. The whole process happened fairly rapidly and was perfectly silent except for our breathing. Then, the screen went blank and nothing happened. We stood frozen. None of us had thought that it would be spectacular, but that it would be definitely better than this.

I couldn't help thinking, "This doesn't work." But, of course, I didn't say it. Experience had taught me that when it came to the twins, only a fool would bet against them when a computer was involved.

"Ah, ha, it didn't work!" David, on the other hand, didn't share my confidence in their skills.

"All that time wasted and it didn't even work." He walked over to Jamal and patted him on the shoulder. "Sorry, man, I thought we'd hooked up with the right people." Shaking his head, he turned to look at us in absolute disdain.

The twins looked at each other; neither had said anything throughout the entire speech David gave. But their faces were strangely active. Paul moved from his position next to Paula, and began to remove the wires she had so painstakingly applied some moments before. Once finished, he turned back toward us and looked David squarely in the eyes.

"You know, only a fool would say an operation didn't take before the procedure was finished," he turned back toward us and looked David squarely in the eyes.

Amazingly, his voice wasn't at all squeaky when he made that statement. His sister beamed at him as he turned back to the safe and pushed one button. The door swung outward.

Now you know the saying about hearing a pin drop? Well I'm sure someone had to have dropped one then. And from the stupid look on David's face, it had to have fallen of top of him. He didn't say anything as he stalked his way out of the room and back up the stairs.

Jamal hesitated and looked after his friend before moving forward with the rest of the gang around the safe. Paul reached in and pulled out a ream of papers professionally bound. He glanced at it briefly then handed it to me.

I began to leaf through it, Jamal and Roberta leaning over each shoulder. Paula stood immediately in front of me, with her back to Paul who was still searching the safe.

"Man, there is a lot of stuff in here." I looked at Ro. "We better take this stuff home." It didn't have "clue" written in italics, but this had to be a break through.

"Found something else." We turned to find Paul, a grin stretched across hi freckled face as he held up a computer disk.

We'd hit pay dirt. Before we could celebrate, there was a yell and bumps from above our heads in what I was sure was the living room. Jamal ran for the stairs. The crew closed ranks. I looked to the twins, and found them looking pretty shaky. I passed the stuff over to Paula.

"Go up the stairs and out the pantry. Turn left and take off out the back door. We'll meet you at my house." They started to say something "Go!" They went.

Ro. and I took up the rear. Paul and Paula went out the back and we went through the alcove into the hall, where we peered around the corner into the living room. The picture we saw was pretty ugly. Two big bruisers each had the arm of one of the guys. The biggest one was definitely the largest man I'd ever seen in my life. He had to have been well over 6′5, with shoulders that must have blocked the light from the sun when outside. The other one was just a smaller version of the same. Granite-carved faces topped with blonde hair completed the picture. Other than that, I can't remember anything else about them. They were just that big and scary.

"Okay, kid, I know you found something. So, give it up." That was the biggest one who had Jamal and was shaking him like my mom shakes out an old dishrag. I went up in flame, not a slow burn, but like a bomb.

"Let's go!" Ro. didn't have a chance to say no. And, actually, the truth is she wanted to get in there as badly as I did. She called for "action plan no.3" and I nodded in agreement.

We jumped up and ran into the room. The four already there froze with almost identical expressions of shock and amazement. Ro. and I landed on our knees in front of the hoods. I had the largest one and she had the one with David.

That's when the yelling in Spanish and crying began. I did the same thing well, except for the Spanish. Tears poured down both our faces. In the shock of the moment, Jamal and David had been released and tried to comfort us. As if we'd practiced this for years we pushed them away and turned in one fluid motion to deliver perfect front fists into the groins of the two men. Next second, we were both on our feet and the men were now the ones on their knees. Ro. slapped me five and we put them away with well placed kicks in the face and chops to the back of the head.

"What, how, who?" David was really having problems with the English language that day. Jamal's look, on the other hand, was very meaningful, so I answered his look.

"Well, my Dad followed Dr. King and believes in nonviolence and tried to teach me and my brothers this way of life without any knowledge of physical violence. While my Mom loved Dr. King, she followed the "By Any Means Necessary" teachings of Malcolm X."

The boys looked at me vacantly, as if I were speaking to them in German or something. So, I put it simply. "Ma has a third degree black belt. She's been teaching Ro. and me since we were old enough to walk. We're not sure, but she says both of us must be black belt caliber at the very least."

"That's not true." Ro. had to put her two cents worth in. "Your mom says you've got your first degree."

"Whatever." The guys started to giggle, probably in shock and nervousness that probably would have ended in hysteria if the thugs hadn't decided to start coming alive with moans and groans of pain.

We flew into action almost stumbling over ourselves to get out of the house. The back door slammed behind us as we had our bikes and were heading toward Mission Avenue. I yelled "If we get split up, meet back at my house. We'll meet back at my house. We'll go over the papers and check out the disks." I know it might sound kind of corny, but we just couldn't resist slapping five and the occasional "Ye, ha!"

I wish I could tell you that there had been an exciting chase, but there wasn't. That, of course, didn't stop us from reenacting every bike chase scene the movies had ever known. As it turns out, that was all for the best.

Chapter 9

Back at the Lewis' house, the henchman managed to pick themselves off the floor with a great deal of foul language. "Dang Bob," the smaller one said as he rubbed his head where a lump was definitely forming.

"What are we gonna tell the boss?"

"Well, Rick, we're going to do what anyone in our position would." i.e. Two grown men sent to nab some kid who ends up getting their butts kicked by two little girls.

"We're going to tell the truth," He took out his handkerchief and wiped blood out from under his left eye. For a second he stared at the blood, then his lips curled into a rueful smile and he looked at his companion. "And we're going to lie our butts off."

Rick rubbed his head in confusion, "How?"

"Just leave it to me." Bob sighed and pulled out his flip phone from an inside pocket of his tailored black business suit. "Yeah, this is Bob. Put me through to the control room." There was a brief pause while he was transferred and he took slow deep breaths to strengthen himself. Rick was glad he hadn't had to make this call. The Boss was going to be angry regardless of the lie that Bob told him.

"Yes, Mr. Dupree, this is Robert." Samuel hated shortened names. "Yes, sir, we did like you told us, but the boy had a friend with him and they kind of caught us by surprise. I don't know what they used on us but we've been out for at least five minutes. When we came to, they were gone." Bob's end of the conversation was over after that. Rick watched him as he flushed, then paled until he was sure that his buddy was going to pass out.

"Yes, sir, Yes, sir," was all Bob could say until he hung up in relief.

"Well?"

"Well, we're supposed to make a thorough search of this joint, and then ride the neighborhood looking for those... kids." Bob removed his jacket exposing a sleeveless T-shirt, his shoulder holster and hair arm pits to the air. He began his search and Rick joined in.

Across town, things weren't nearly as calm. Samuel replaced the receiver and slowly, yet resolutely, began to tear the phone apart.

Behind him, Wendal shook and tears of fear actually ran down his face. He was more afraid of this whirling dervish of destruction than he'd ever been. And although all of that was true, a small kernel of hope began to get larger within the heart of that little man. For surely, whatever could cause this much anger could mean nothing but good for him.

Samuel turned from the small pieces of gears and plastic that were the remains of the phone. His hair was wild; his clothes were askew; and there was an even wilder look in his eyes.

"It seems there is more going on here than we'd thought at first." He began to put himself back together, straightening his tie, jacket and shirt. "Prepare the Lewis's for questioning. We need to know what that brat of theirs might have found that we don't already have." He began to comb his hair. "But, most importantly, where we can find him." When he'd finished his grooming session, he brushed past Wendal and headed for the door. Turning with his hand on the door, he said "make sure you clean this place up," Like nothing had ever happened.

Chapter 10

(In my room.)

Beep. Whir. Beep Whir. It had been going on for what had seemed like forever. Night was long past having fallen. It was about 7 o'clock and we'd been deciphering the code both in the book and on the disk. We broke it first in the book, which helped with the computer. The language was very simple, so the last half an hour had gone very quickly. I asked Jamal why it wasn't more complicated.

"Mom and Pop didn't believe in talkin' down to people." He shrugged and kept turning pages. No one spoke for a while. We read and reread. We flipped pages and scrolled down the computer screen. What began to unfold was so frightening none of us wanted to be the one to say the words. Once again, it was left to me. Dang, this strong leader stuff was really starting to work on my nerves.

"All right, I'll start us off." Everyone stopped what they were doing, which was only pretending to be deep in thought anyway; and oriented themselves in my direction. The twins turned from the computer inside Grandpa's roll top desk to look expectantly toward my bed where the rest of us were sitting. I was leaning against the headboard of my bed with Roberta immediately to my right. Jamal and David were half kneeling, half sitting, one on each side of the end of the bed.

Throwing the papers on the floor, I sat back with a loud bang. Yes, it did hurt but I didn't mind the pain. "Since no one wants to go first," I rubbed my eyes from exhaustion and frustration. "If these papers have anything they want to tell me, they better sprout some lips and make it plain." The bubble of tension burst at my sarcastic remark, and my old friends grinned at each other and at me. I guess I have my uses, too.

Ro. said something under her breath. I don't know what, but I elbowed her anyway.

"Do something." David said urgently.

"What can I do?" I didn't mean to, but it came out more like a scream than a question.

At the computer, Paula and Paul wore identical expressions filled with shame and embarrassment.

"Any luck with the disk?" I was reaching for the stars. Grabbing at anything for hope. I was just wasting time. I knew if they'd found anything we'd have known way before now.

Paula spoke up. "Sure," she blushed. "We broke the code. Piece of cake. The only problem is, we have no idea what the formulae and equations mean." All eyes were on them, and the twins moved closer to each other. Paul took over the explanation. "We do computers, not chemistry." Mumbled apologies came from us all and they turned back to the computer.

"The only thing we do understand is this letter." That got our attention, and we moved to take positions behind them so we could read over their shoulders.

What we saw was a letter from Jamal's parents to the Secretary of Defense. The letter talked about the deterilous side effects of something called X 15. The last line says that the hypothesis was correct, but the side effects heavily out-weighted the benefits and they strongly advised against it.

X 15. Secretary of Defense

Everyone started talking at once. Someone said this was more than they had expected. My head begun to hurt a long time before, and the jumble of voices only increased the volume of the hammers pounding away in my head. There was no help for it, I was officially the leader therefore it was up to me to get things back on track. I had to rest first so I sat down with my back leaning against the foot of the bed with my knees pulled in tightly to my chest. They stopped talking and arranged themselves around me.

"Time to huddle." The twins and Ro. moved in closer, but Jamal and David just sat there blinking like owls in strong light.

"Look, guys, I know you know what huddle means." Can you tell I was losing any semblance of patience, which I have in short supply anyway. One more angry look from me and they moved into space left for them by the others.

We argued and fought for another half-an-hour, but this is all that came out.

> 1. Dangerous bad guys.
> 2. Jamal's parents in very real danger.
> 3. Something had to be done.
> 4. We needed help.

Up to this point, we'd all pretty much been of one mind. "Did you pay close attention to the, we'd?" Which means, we had? I hope so, because what comes next still has the power to give me a serious headache.

5. Call the Police.

That's when the fights seriously broke out. It got really ugly. The twins, strangely enough, were on the side of nonconformity. They felt that although the situation was serious and dangerous to boot, we didn't have enough evidence to be believed by the police. Man, those twins can really blow my mind.

David and Jamal were on the side of "No" and I quote "Cop calling 'cause they didn't know what they were doing half the time anyway." This was followed by a silence almost eerie in its suddenness, especially since I was only half-listening anyway until he had opened his mouth.

I looked over at him, and he at least had the courtesy to look away in embarrassment.

"If you two are finished," I said to Jamal and his mouth-impaired friend, "its Ro.'s turn." Ro. was of a mind to call my Mom and Dad and dump the whole thing in their laps "where it should have been in the first place." This was directed partially toward me, but mostly at David who frowned back; but who hadn't recovered enough to look at me.

As she wound down breathlessly and sat back, my turn had come. Throughout the discussion and arguments, I'd been silent except when I was needed to play facilitator. So, now I felt the weight of their expectations lying heavily on my shoulders.

I looked into each pair of eyes in turn and knew I needed help. Not the help of the Police, although the thought of Mom and Pop were nearly enough to send me into tears, but a specialist was what I needed. Someone who could help me find my direction; who wouldn't step in and force me to take it. There was only one person who fit the bill, Mrs. Gutierrez.

"What time is it?" I asked with my head on my knees. David checked his watch, "10:30." There were gasps from everyone.

"Okay, I say we postpone anymore discussion, or decisions for that matter, until tomorrow morning at ten in the tower." There were nods all around. The twins needed to call and let their Dad know they were on the way home. Their house was the closest thing I had ever seen to maximum security. So, if they didn't call, they wouldn't be able to get to the door without alerting the National Guard in three states.

I struck my head in my parent's room and told Pop I'd be just a little bit and walked with everyone else out the door and down the stairs. It was a fresh-smelling night with a sky blue and sparkly like dark blue velvet sprinkled with diamonds.

Paul and Paula said good night in unison and trotted off down Hicks Street to Higgins, which is just a couple of blocks away.

Jamal and David left a little slower but they too walked away toward David's apartment building with much discussion still going on. (Mostly from David, of course, sometimes I think he couldn't follow directions if his life depended on it.)

All I could hope was that it never would.

"Well, Amiga, I suppose now is not the time for explanations either, eh?" It was my turn to be relieved. I had been dreading this moment all day. No one had asked about what I could do or about the things I had done. If Jamal or David or for that matter even the twins had asked I wouldn't have told them anything. But Ro. was different. We were closer than some sisters and I'd never told her this one secret. Our history made it okay for her to ask, and expect an honest thorough answer. But she had known that the time was all wrong for the heart to heart we both needed. So she let me off the hook. I gave her a quick hug goodnight and watched as she opened her door and was enveloped by the warm sounds and good smells waiting for her and me whenever I let myself take part. I was always welcome.

The Martinez house was a familiar as my own, but I had a problem to solve, and there was only one person who could help. I skirted the stairs and walked around the side facing Dubuque Street to where a rickety, green fence creaked and swayed in the sweet night breeze.

Chapter 11

Wendal finally looked up from the floor, after both the Lewis's had been dragged from their chairs and out of the circle of light. Tears had poured from his eyes as the two scientists had been questioned from early in the afternoon until now, just a few minutes before ten at night.

When the two nearly - silent men began explaining to the two Doctors what was to be done to them, Wendal had hoped that the Lewis's would have some shred of self-preservation. The atrocities would be many, they had been told, and much, much more. More and more. And the only hope of relief they were given would come when they gave up the information required.

The two skilled purveyors of pain had become amazed by the grit and fortitude displayed. They could not comprehend the motive that kept the Lewis's from talking. Having no children, or anyone else for that matter, parental love and protection went beyond their limited understanding. Wendal understood. In some deep corner of his mind, he remembered having children once. Not clear memory, but the sort of foggy, misty memory that people sometimes have when their remembrances give them more pain than joy. He knew and he was proud and ashamed, to have witnessed what happened in that room. Proud they hadn't told what they had been asked. Yet ashamed of being associated with the people who were heaping discomfort on these two extraordinary individuals. He was ashamed, and resolved - resolved to act when the time was right, not yet, but soon. And afterward, Samuel Dupree would be no one's master, not even his own!

Almost as if thinking about him called him up, he appeared. He stepped into the light, pulling elegantly on his ever-present brown cigarette with his lips.

"In..teresting." He exhaled the word as he circled the two chairs and came to a stop in front of Wendal.

"What is this?" He leaned closer and closer and stared intently at Wendal's face. He didn't notice that for once Wendal wasn't shaking, so intent was he on inspecting the tracks tears had left on Wendal.

"How amazing, tears for someone other than yourself." He studied Wendal like he was a scientific experiment. Like a new germ under the electron microscope.

Dupree turned from Wendal, continuing to rub the oily tear between thumb and forefinger. He walked from the light into the surrounding darkness, throwing over his shoulder as he left, "Have Bob and Rick continue surveillance at the Lewis house in addition to regular sweeps their men are making all over the city" He paused a moment, half-in and half-out of the light. Someone who didn't know better would have misinterpreted his beautiful gentle smile. Not Wendal. Samuel brushed an imaginary speck of dirt from the lapel of his ultra white suit. When he looked up, the mask was gone and his face was hard enough to cut stone from the ground up.

"Make Sure they comprehend the depths my disappointment can go." Then he was gone. Wendal didn't move for the phone until after the sharp click of well-polished (Ashley Martins) receded into the dark.

Chapter 12

Warm air pushed the masks and figures dangling from the lattice work on the roof of Mrs. G's partially - enclosed garden. In the light, I would have seen bright colors and happy smiling faces of some of the guardians that hung from the ceiling and surrounded the walls. Rose bushes were so old that they had a personality and presence that wouldn't allow tampering by the neighborhood flower thieves.

People were wary of the garden and of Mrs. G, herself. They gathered together and "accidentally" began discussing her whenever she worked in her garden or walked to the little grocery store down the street rather than taking the bus to the big store where everyone else went. Without understanding why, they were afraid, they stepped around her very carefully.

I understood the reason they were afraid, it was the same reason I wasn't. She practiced the mystic arts. Divination, Astrology, potions, signs and symbols. You name it, and she did it. Excuse me, if it was bound to the spirits of the land she did it. In other words, she was a witch. She listened to the wind for wisdom and bowed to the four corners for her strength. She also prayed to God, just to be sure all her bases were covered, and crossed herself as any devout Catholic would. Except, she wouldn't attend mass, because it was inside and away from the gifts of God and the land.

The short trek through Mrs. G's jungle took a moment or two, then I was through her screened-in porch and at her door. Mrs. G. didn't stand on ceremony, I just didn't stand on ceremony, so I just opened the door and walked in. As expected, there was a fire blazing in the fire place, welcoming me into the room.

A warm furry body wrapped itself around my ankle. I reached down and untangled "Hat" from my leg and brought the most autocratic and beautiful black cat the world has ever known.

"Good evening your majesty." I addressed her when she was high enough to see my eyes. Hers were a frosty green and with the intelligence of the African Queen from whom she got her name, Hatshepsut. She sniffed delicately at me before she snuggled into my arms and began to purr.

"So, Chile, she remembers you now." The voice came from the old wooden rocker sitting to the side of the fire place. "Come on in, we been expecting you." I moved and the boards beneath my feet popped and cracked, marking my passage from door to fireplace. A hand-woven rug placed at the foot of the rocker was my seat. Usually Hat. and I fight over this prize spot. Tonight for the first time we shared. (Another hint that this was going to require as much support as I could get. Did I listen? No.) We settled down and I turned, pressing my back against the legs that had been waiting for me. Strong hands began to take down my braids, and the voice began to hum softly in patois.

Mrs. Gutierrez is Jamaican. She met Mr. G. at a flea market one day and she bullied him into marrying her the next. Neither of them ever had any regrets. He was gone now. He passed winter before last, and my mom sort of took Mrs. G under her wing. For me, it was like love at first sight. She became sister, confidant, Grandmother, story teller and keeper of our histories, our Griot. But, to me she was even more. She was my teacher. When I started having problems she understood and tried to guide me through the rough spots; at least, as best she could. I'm kinda hardheaded after all. What we discovered was that if she braided my hair it had a soothing affect on both of us, so she could get further in her teaching.

She hummed this night as I slowly told her about the situation my friends and I faced. My story finished as she ended the last braid in my hair and turned me around to face her. Mrs. G's warm brown face was young looking, but old at the same time. Not smooth, it was well-lined and grooved with experience. She wore her dreded locks down and around her shoulders and chest. As usual, she was in black, her color of power. Many people feel that black is a sinister color. Mrs. G. says that black reminds her of the rich earth in which farmers plant their fields and from those fields spring every color in the rainbow.

Briefly, I wondered what color she wore today, because although the color on the outside stayed the same, her moods had a color. So, her mood became the color she wore.

Crossing her long thin arms across her ample chest, she began to rock slowly. Brown eyes smiled down at me and she said, "Oh, Chile, I knew sometin' was happenin' out der wit you dis night." She stared into the fire and far away expression that always managed to send chills down my spine covered her face. When next she spoke, her voice was changed.

"You're, afraid of your destiny Kanya Iska (Hausa for Ebony wind), don't worry and do as the wind guides you." Mrs. Gutierrez blinked rapidly and she was back to normal- well, normal for her.

She smiled again at me and shifted forward in her chair. Her matted, nearly braid - like dreds spilled over her arms as she reached to touch my face. "Honey Girl, I know you is afraid, but your gift be from God above. Dis' your job and it was goin' to begin sooner or later."

I was pulled toward her with just the tips of her fingers, and kissed firmly on each check and my forehead. Each kiss was symbolic of something, the two on my cheeks were of welcome and also goodnight. The one she'd planted on my forehead was one of older sister to younger, reminding me that she was just a thought away.

I let myself out and Hat walked me to the gate. The warm breeze that had come with me was still here, but turned slightly cold and chilled me. The moon was still full, just as beautiful as the night before, except now I knew what it had been trying to tell me yesterday. Destiny calls.

I took no comfort in the understanding I'd been gifted with. I knew what I had to go and do tomorrow. I also knew, as I crept into my house, that for the second night in a row I would get little to no sleep.

Chapter 13

Next morning found me on the 7:00 A.m. bus to Buddy Todd Park. Mrs. G had been right last night or really early this morning. I had known what to do. I had to go back to Jamal's house. But, this time I needed to be there alone. While I appreciated the company of my friends, they clouded the impressions I might be able to get from the place. Time passed, I exited the bus and after a short walk found myself standing alone outside the door to the house. It occurred to me suddenly that I didn't have a key to get into the house. I called myself a few ugly names and almost walked away. On impulse, I reached for the door knob and gave it a bit of a turn. The door opened without a sound and I was drawn into the darkness of the interior once again, but this time alone.

The door slammed closed without any help from me. Pictures flew at me with the closing of that door, like a floodgate opening. It was almost too much, and I had to use the staircase to support myself while I struggled to contain the images threatening to bring me to my knees. Slowly, my breathing came under my control and I was able to stand without support. The images had not stopped. I'd just slowed them enough so that they were coming one at a time instead of all at once.

Scenes of loving family life; Good times bad times; Jamal's first steps were taken in this house, and I was watching him take them; The day-to-day living of years was mine to view. Time passed quickly until I came to more recent events; the Doctors Lewis working on the secret project and the disturbing phone calls that Jamal had told us about. I saw their stress and their worry. Lastly, I saw the Scabs the Doctors Lewis had been replaced with and the fight, our fight, of the afternoon before.

The flow stopped and I checked my watch and found that I had just ten minutes to catch the bus that would get me to the tower in time to meet with my friends. Using five of those minutes, I made a quick search of the living room in hopes that one of the thugs had left a clue. Like a note with letter head or a match box with tell-tale materials that would give me a clue as to where to find Jamal's parents. Things like that always seem to happen to my favorite detectives of T.V. and in books. Giving the sleuth the clue they needed to wrap up the mystery in time for a group denouncement following tea and crumpets. It happens like that all the time, but did it happen like that for me? Yeah, right. It would have to be harder than that for me.

I left that house feeling more frustrated than I had before I got there. After making sure I'd locked up, I tore down the street in hopes that I hadn't missed my bus. That's probably why I didn't see the low black sedan that had just turned the corner, trailing behind me as I jumped onto the bus and paid my fare.

Chapter 14

The bus I'd transferred on to let me off on 6th Street, where I walked down to the Strand. It wasn't a long walk, but it was plenty long enough for me to kick myself over and over again. I know that there was nothing for me to find which is why I didn't find anything. But, what was I going to tell the others? It was my responsibility and I had failed. Before I knew it, the door of the tower was in front of me.

I moved to open it, but my hand never reached the handle. I was snatched into the gloom, bringing me face to face with an angry Roberta.

"Where have you been!" She didn't give me a chance to think up a good lie. "You went to Jamal's, didn't ya?" Her cheeks flushed and her eyes began to water.

"Oh, Ro., I'm sorry." I was well and truly shocked for the first time that day. I reached out for my friend and we hugged like we haven't hugged each other in three years. That's when we'd decided that we were women and had to behave in a certain way in public, never mind that since then we've been in enough fights, with each other and people in the neighborhood we couldn't begin to count them.

She was genuinely upset and she was shaking in my arms. Lord have Mercy! She'd been afraid for me. Over Ro,' shoulder my eye's met Jamal's.

"She started to worry about an hour ago," he hesitated, "We told her that you were probably just checkin' on a hunch or something like that. But she wouldn't hear it, said that you wouldn't have gone without letting someone know where you were." He looked from me to Roberta and back to me again before shaking his head and moving to the far side of the room, leaving my Bud and I standing in front of the still-open door.

I keep a scrap of cloth on me for the occasional intense moments in my life, so I pulled it out of my back pocket and stuffed it in Ro.'s hand. She was getting back her control enough that she was mumbling bad things about me under her breath in Spanish, as I led her to the crate on the back wall.

Suddenly, I was overtaken by a wave of nervous energy and I paced the five feet between the door and the back wall as I explained my whereabouts.

"I had to go back there." I paused to look around at the faces surrounding me, Jamal, David, the twins and, of course, Ro. who I looked at last of all. "Sorry I worried you." The tension overtook me and I began to pace again. "I know better and there is no excuse for it."

I stopped on the side of the opened door and pressed my shoulder against the wall so I could stare out, at the waves and the surfers, trying to find the inner peace the ocean has always given me before. More solace was to be found in the cool, yet splintery wood where I rested my cheek in near despair.

"I was sure if I went there alone I'd find something useful, something that we missed last time or that might have been dropped when we hauled tail outta there." It was my turn to get totally choked up. But when David said, "Well, did you find anything?" It was the last straw. I took the necessary steps to bring me outside so the tears could roll down my face in peace. I hate crying. I suppose it's because I'm not a beautiful crier. My face swells up, my nose runs like crazy and instead of bird-like hiccups and gasps; gut-wrenching, deep-throated sobs croak from my mouth. So, I try to do it as little as possible. Besides, with a reputation like mine, you have to be tougher than your average person. Okay, so maybe I'm exaggerating, but only a little.

A hand dropped on my shoulder, stopping my tears in mid - croak. It was Jamal, I knew before I started to turn that he'd come to give me whatever comfort he could. Out of the corner of my eye, something caught my attention. Quickly, I turned back to Jamal, catching him off guard when I planted my hand firmly in the center of his chest and pushed him backward into the tower. Following him in I slammed the door behind me. The locking mechanism had long since rusted away. So Ro. and I had improvised a bar and the slats that did a pretty good job of keeping people out when we were inside. Right now, there were people coming who really needed to be kept out.

My eyes swept the room, and my friends, who came to help Jamal from the floor, stared back at me. I suppose that my psychic energy had gone off the scale. They told me later that they could almost see sparks flying off me. It's possible, I can't say, things happened kind of quickly after that.

"They're out there." my voice was calm and controlled.

"Who's out there?" The twins said in unison. You know for some reason their unison didn't faze me at all.

"Those thugs from yesterday." Straight to the point.

David and Jamal both began to panic. "Dang, Dang, Dang." I don't remember who said it, but they both rushed to the cracks on the south facing wall to verify what I'd said. "Dang," after they caught sight of those two crossing the sand.

David turned back in time to see us pushing the crate aside, and there was finally real fear in his eyes. "That thing isn't nearly heav.." he stopped when Roberta removed the two by two foot square from the wall that the crate had always hidden. No, I didn't mention our little back door. Ro. and I had secretly put it in the year we'd found the tower. For some reason, we knew that, like the cross bar on the door, this, too, would come in handy. Only a few of our closest friends knew about it, so why would I tell you before you needed to know?

Paula was first out, followed closely by Paul and David. Jamal hung back. I suppose it was his chivalrous streak perking up. Women and children first and all that stuff. Unfortunately for him, Ro. and I weren't havin' none of that. I enlightened him.

"Look, get outta here." Yes, once again, short and to the point. After all, the thugs would be here at any second if not sooner. As if the thought of them called their ugly butts into being, there came a very polite knock on the door. Followed by a clearing of a throat more frightening than most of the stuff that has happened so far. I don't know why, but it really bent all of us out of shape.

"Excuse me," said a temporarily gentle voice on the other side of the door. "Jamal, we just want to talk to you and your friends. That's all."

There was silence as we digested them calling Jamal by name. We motioned him to the bolt hole. He shook his head furiously and I scuttled across the floor on my knees to where he was and put my face really close to his ear. Even with all the tension in the air, I still took a second to notice that it was nicely shaped as ears go, and, most importantly, it was clean.

"You know about how the captain of a ship goes down with it when it sinks?" He frowned at me but nodded yes anyway. "We're not going to do anything stupid like that." He smiled and actually started to say something. Our eyes stared into each other. I don't know what he was thinking, and to be honest I'm still not sure what I was thinking either.

His smile deepened, then it was my turn to frown. Ro. hissed at me, bringing me back to reality.

"We're not goin' down with this sinking ship, but we're definitely the first ones to make it ours, so we'll be the last to leave it!" Finally he got it, he ducked his head and squirmed through the opening.

Once he was through, Ro. and I started digging at the sand to the north of the opening. Sand flew everywhere. Our hands touched the box at the same moment someone tested the strength of the door.

"Creak, Pop." but the door and our bar held their own. Our bodies went into automatic, almost as if we'd practiced this moment one hundred or more times. Actually, we had practiced. Like I said before, we always kind o' expected something like this. Ro. went first and I followed after sweeping my eyes around this small room that had meant a lot to all my friends, but most of all to Ro. and me. For some reason I was certain that I'd never see it again.

The solid thud of shoulder against wood set me back into motion. And I backed out the hole, pulling the crate back in place, then the paneling as well. Heading south, I followed the small ravine I had crawled into, moving as silently as I possibly could.

Loosely packed dirt from the walls fell down on my head and roots from vines tried to grab me as I scrambled past. A loud crack, followed by a lot of cussing behind me, stopped me in my tracks. Then, they started turning over what little stuff there was. I was just five feet away and the sound was reaching me very clearly.

I inched my way forward, barely breathing, till I came to the real drainage ditch that was my destination. I looked up, checking to make sure that my enemies were still behind me. Ro. was nowhere to be seen (that girl was fast). I started up the concrete tube that was protected on two sides by climbing vines and overhanging fern. I quickened my pace a little bit.

We'd been without rain for at least two months, so there was nothing slimy waiting for my hands and knees as I moved closer and closer to the top. Half-way up, something made me look back. Tendrils of smoke greeted my eyes and stabbed my heart. The two men walked away slowly, trying not to draw attention to themselves. It worked, because no one noticed the smoke until the thugs reached their car. I suppose that anger had caused them to burn our place, anger and a need to hurt us somehow. They were successful in that, if in no other way. I was most definitely hurt. Tears poured down my face, but my mind was clear and strengthened with the pain. Flipping over, I was out of the ditch before I even knew that was what I was doing. Fortunately, nobody had been looking at where I'd come out. I probably would have scared them to death. I came out running. Weaving my way through cars, I began to develop a plan which I'd completed by the time I'd met up with the rest of the crew at the end of 6th Street, where they were waiting at the circular drive that separated one end of the Strand from the other.

Chapter 15

The thugs stood and watched as the police questioned the closest sun bathers, and the fire department picked through the still - smoking building. I mean, what was left of the building.

We'd been watching too, from the seats built into the short decorative wall that formed a half moon around the road. It wasn't too risky a place for us to be watching from. Besides, those two idiots were having too much fun watching the Police and the fire departments do their work.

"This is the plan," Everyone turned from the spectacle to sit facing me. "Ro. we need Enrique." She was shocked. Enrique was one of my least favorite people in the world. He'd tormented me for the better part of five years. And to say I hated him, most of the time, was putting it mildly. When I see Enrique and his friends coming, I cross the street. That tell you anything? At this point it's not necessary for me to go in to the why's and the where-fors of Enrique's and my "relationship". I'll explain it during another adventure, if there are anymore.

"All right, Ro. you better take off and call Enrique. I'll fill you in on our way home." She took of at a run without any questions. I suppose it was the excitement of the moment. I fully expected to hear about me ordering her around, but not for a little while.

The wind picked up, bringing with it the noises of the lookie-loo's behind us. Camera crews were beginning to arrive. Those guys wouldn't be going anywhere for at least another half hour. The news team's arrival insured it, because even if they weren't completely fascinated with the goings on, which they were, the parking lot was now at capacity. Leaving beach goers with nothing to do but park their cars anywhere they could. And fortunately for us, anywhere turned out to be behind someone else's car.

We waited for a while, quite enjoying the way the two thus yelled and screamed at each other, once they'd discovered their predicament, and then at anyone else who stopped and got in the way.

Twenty minutes passed swiftly, until an incredibly tooled-out low rider came down the hill and around the island of transplanted palms to pull up in front of us. Window tinted just a shade less than legal rolled down and Ro. peered out at us between the press of beefy shoulders.

Doors opened and five of the toughest looking home boys you've ever seen stepped out. The roughest looking one exited from the driver's side and came over to stand looking down at me. He was very close. I put my hand on his chest and pushed him back a step. This was followed by a burst of masculine chuckling and pushing amongst the other guys who'd come with my adversary.

Dark lenses stared down at me. This was Enrique. Black cap, shirt, pants and shoes plus a brand new black mustachio that Roberta says he's been nursing like a baby.

"Okay, Nina, what you need me for?" He grinned in a secret, sly kind of way. That's the problem we have with each other. You see, Enrique's irresistible to females the world over. Unfortunately, I must have been asleep when the spell was released because he does nothing for me. I guess it kind of bugs him, so he does everything he possibly can to get in my face. This time it would work in my favor, because Enrique and his friends were heavily into their role-playing games and running around shooting each other when they go paint balling. That's how they spend their time when they're not working or in school. It would take something pretty important to drag them away, I guess I should be flattered. Nope!

I just gave it to him in one long rush, without taking a breath and finished with, "and we need you to tail those two guys over there." I pointed over his shoulder at the two under discussion. He didn't even turn around to see who I was pointing at, he just continued to star hard at me. I looked away from his eyes, trying to look at anyone but him. Everyone was quiet. As if they could tell that whatever was happening was pretty important, so that even though it had to have been killing them, this was just too essential a meeting to interrupt.

An obnoxious horn drew my attention back to the parking lot and our friend, the goon squad. Of course, the noise was coming from them. They'd given up trying to talk people into moving. They were now using a more direct approach.

This new method consisted of honking constantly as you drove slowly forward in a daring move that reminded me of a game of chicken played at slow speed. Oh yeah, it worked. There was a great deal of yelling and screaming, but if we didn't act soon they'd be gone before I could put my plan in action. I knew what Enrique was waiting for, I just didn't want to do it.

He just stood there, enjoying my dilemma, I could tell by the look in his eyes.

"Please." My teeth clenched so hard that I touched my mouth to make sure I wasn't bleeding.

He smiled and signaled behind him to his friends, who quickly climbed back into the car. Enrique checked over his shoulder and made visual contact with the car he'd been asked to tail. The car was steadily drawing nearer to escaping the bonds of the parking lot.

Enrique turned back to me, "Better get undercover before you get spotted." We all sort of jumped, because of course that had been the last thought on any of our minds. We all turned to scramble over the low wall directly behind us. And of course, Enrique stopped me before I could make it over. "Remember you owe me." He dropped the hand that had grabbed me and sauntered around to the driver's side.

He gave me the sassiest wave possible before he disappeared behind the wheel.

Without realizing I'd done it, I found myself on the other side of the wall face down in the sand. All I could think of was the trouble I'd managed to get myself into. I was told later that I was making strange little sounds, before a car engine sent us scurrying to the end of the wall. We caught glimpses as our improvised deputies fell in behind Thug#1 and Thug #2. For a second, I feared Enrique would get too close and they'd be made, but I had no real reason to worry. (Not that I needed a real reason.) They were gamers of the highest quality. The kind that begin on a board in someone's car port, then progress to the point where the game becomes closer to reality-war games, survivalist training. Their car paused just a moment longer than anyone else's at the top of the hill before easing cautiously out into traffic. They wouldn't be lost or discovered easily, this was one of their favorite games.

A lone seagull's cry sent chills down my spine and drew my eyes back to the ocean and the deepening colors of the sky. If I didn't move quickly, I would be frozen by fear. I started up the hill heading for home, and my friends both old and new fell into step around me. Without breaking stride, I started giving instructions.

"All right, guys, let's split up." Before they could argue, I continued. "Call every kid you know. Tell them to call everyone they know." We reached the top of the hill and paused automatically to catch our breath. Behind us the roar of the ocean dwindled next to the importance of the things to which we all had to come to terms. In our crew, when things got tough we joined our forces and drew closer for support. I know it's kind of corny, but we held hands; we needed that comfort more now than ever before. Spontaneously, we moved together, pulling Jamal and David into our circle. We examined each others eyes, checking to see how serious we all were about what we were ultimately up against.

I looked around and saw fear but much more determination. I can't say what they saw in me, but I know I hoped they couldn't see the dread lying in the pit of my stomach.

"Get home as quickly as possible. Call everyone you can think of and put them on alert. Before this is over, we're going to need them all." Nods all around. "We'll meet at my house as soon as you're done."

Jamal and David slapped five and ran off yelling something about catching someone before practice was over.

The rest of us headed back to Dubuque Street at a steady jog. I took one last look at the seagull and envied him his freedom.

Chapter 16

*T*wo hours have passed and we're all together in my room. The reports had been favorable so far. Everyone we'd contacted were on the alert. I'm not sure why, but everyone was ready and willing to be involved in whatever went down, the rougher the better.

Jamal and David were still being mysterious about what team's practice they'd interrupted. About the only thing they'd say was, "They're ready," with knowing grins for each other. I guess the twins aren't the only irritating people I know.

All the information had come in the first hour we'd gotten back. Since then, we'd all been trying to pretend that the hands on my clock were moving in slow motion or that the phone was getting louder and louder in it's silence with every passing second.

Finally it rang, freezing us all into place. It rang again. Then again. I heard one of my little brothers pick it up, and I listened through the opened door of my room. Then little brother Kwasi poked his sly head around the corner. "Ke Ke,

— 99 —

telephone." He drew the last word out and twisted it just enough to make an older sister wish to be an only child.

"It's a boy.y.y." This time he ended with loud kissy noises, crossed eyes and his arms rapped around his body doing strange things to his back.

Jumping from the bed and charging the door, I sent him screeching down the hall at breakneck speed.

Ro. had already picked up the phone and was talking very quickly to her cousin. I understood most of the conversation, although it was happening very fast and in Spanish. I waited until the call was ended and let Ro. give us all the news at the same time.

"Enrique says that they're at the Del Rio industrial park in one of the big warehouses way in the back. He says there is a lot of moving around of trucks and loading stuff, pretty much non-stop." She looked over at Jamal before continuing. "Looks like they're pulling out. He believes that they've about an hour or so more before the place is empty, two hours max."

Jamal's shoulders had started to slump, David moved to him and the two of them started their usual whispering. Part of me wanted to go to Jamal and comfort him too. I firmly kicked that part in the gut and told her we had business to attend to. Okay, so that's psycho. I don't care.

Grabbin' Ro. by the arm, I pulled her and signaled the twins into the hall.

"Get down to Ro.'s and call everyone you called before and have them meet us at the industrial park in about an hour." They turned to go. "Oh yeah, tell em' to bring every flash light, and all the eggs, toilet paper, and shavin' cream they can get their hands on." Strange as it may seem, they asked no question, just nodded and took off.

Command, you gotta love it.

Jabaree came running around the corner from the living room, followed closely by a broom-wielding Kwasi. He hit somewhere around about the waist, but before I could yell he was behind me and trying to climb my back like a tree. Suddenly the wind stirred in front of my face, and a flash of yellow sped toward my eyes. I was saved only by years of training and a great deal of luck. My arm came up and blocked the broom handle which still landed on my forearm with a loud crack.

"Ow!" came from the soles of my feet to the top of my head. When I was finally able to clear the water from my eyes, I found myself still standing. Well, if you say standing is bent in half with my poor nearly-broken arm protectively pressed against my stomach.

Two sweet little faces peered up at me, from the floor where they'd be in the best position to be seen once my "fit" had ended. Their eyes were wide and Amazed, with just the right touch of innocence. I swear to you I heard heavenly hosts begin to sing. That is until Jabaree started laughing and slapped his mouth closed with his hand. Kwasi's mouth rounded like a little brown and red "o", and he added his hand to his brothers. Moral support, ya' know? Kwasi started yelling after his ungrateful brother sank his teeth into his hand. If I hadn't picked that moment to regain the ability to speak, I know they would've been at it again.

"You little demon spawn," They stopped between one push and a really good shove. The picture would have been really funny if the memory of that broom and my arm wasn't still a painful reality. My mind shuttled through all my torture options and had narrowed it down to my two favorites, dangling by the ankles until they passed out, or stripping them naked and forcing them to run around in the weeds of the canyon.

It was not to be, because Jamal and David came out of the room behind me. Movement to my left brought my attention in that direction. Jamal squatted beside me and said, "Are you okay."

With his asking, suddenly I was. I nodded and began to unfold myself. Rising in unison once again we found ourselves lost in each other's eyes. I could say that not much time passed while we stared at each other, but if I did it would be a lie. An hour could have sped by for all the care the two of us would have given it.

A small hand tugging on my arm saved me, and brought me back to reality. I looked down at Kwasi's jealous little face and something important finally occurred to me. "My parents aren't home!" David and Jamal just sort of shrugged my statement away. I said it again,

"My....Parents....aren't....home....!" I slowed it down so their brains could catch on. It didn't work. Finally I raised the hand that Kwasi was still clutching possessively, Jamal's and

David's heads went back and forth between me and Kwasi. Until finally "Bing" (I swear to you I heard that sound) the light of understanding shone in their eyes.

I dragged a reluctant five year old into the living room, where he proceeded to throw one of the most spectacular fits in history, which I ignored. He calmed a bit while I got to the phone and dialed.

"Oceanside Police Department, Captain Renfrow speaking. Is this and emergency?" The voice on the other end was deep and familiar.

"Uncle Bob?" he coughed, "Keisha, I hope your not playin', hon, you know this is the official line and all calls are monitored."

"Be Quiet!" to my little brother whose noise finally cut through everything else. A modified shriek could be heard on the other end, "No, sir, not you Uncle Bob. I mean Officer Renfrow. I was talking to Kwasi. He's having a conniption fit right here next to me."

"All right, so what can I help you with?" By the tone of his voice I could tell he had decided that this was some kind of a game, regardless of my assurances. I could almost hear him thinking, sweet little Keisha. I didn't have time to be offended by his condescending attitude, besides it was going to be a help to me. So, although I thought the world of my adopted Uncle Bob, I had no problem with taking advantage of his trusting nature.

"Can you get a message to either my Mom or Dad?"

"KeKe, what's going on?"

"Why nothin', my friends and I have some place to go so, Jabaree and Kwasi will be next door at Mrs. Gutierrez's. Just in case." That last part slid out before I could stop it.

"Just in case what, what's going on?" My eyes crossed and I thought really hard. Nothin'. There was only one thing to do. Lie and run.

"Oh, Uncle Bob, gotta go, oh, stop it you two. The boys are fighting again." Just to prove it I gave the obnoxiously quiet Kwasi a pinch hard enough to start him screaming. "Bye, gotta go. Make sure Mom and Dad get my message. Thanks." The click of the receiver cut Officer Robert Renfrow off in mid - question. I later found out that the shock of being ignored by me, set him into immediate action. So that with in ten minutes of my call, he had notified both my parents on opposite sides of town. And they, knowing me, also rolled into action.

But, like I said that's stuff I found out later.

I hugged Kwasi and apologized for the pinch and explained to both him and Jabaree that they would have to play in Mrs. G's yard for a while because I had something very important I need to do. My two little brothers were very quiet as I got them ready to go. So quiet that I asked them what was wrong as we walked out the door that I locked behind us. Jabaree answered. His sweet face looked up at me with brown eyes so much like my mom's, and he was so worried that I bent quickly and hugged him close.

"Don't go," he whispered into my ear.

"I'll be okay Baree, I promise."

"You promise?"

"I promise." Both David and Jamal looked a question at me that I answered with a frown and a shake of my head. I know I'd made a promise that I couldn't possibly be sure I could keep. But, these were my baby brothers and although I pride myself on never having lied to them, I hoped it wouldn't matter if it kept them from being afraid. No, it doesn't work for me either, but what can you do?

Anyway, they clung tightly to my sides as we came down the stairs past all of our bikes and then turned left to Mrs. G's gate. Hat met us at the gate with the slow rolling stride of a panther and following close behind came Mrs. G. Her hair was wrapped tall on her head and she wore the black robes she said helped her gather her spirit. Her feet were bare except for gold rings on her toes that matched rings on two of her fingers. Her spirit reached out for me as she opened the gate to Jabaree and Kwasi, who found extra energy as they crossed the threshold and took off after a playful Hat without a backward glance for me. Yes, it hurt my feelings being forgotten so quickly, but Mrs. G understood and laughed at me.

"Oh, Chile, I thought you didn't want dem' to worry. So I made a special spell just for da' two wee mens." She smiled gently and took me in her arms and kissed me on my forehead. "For luck," she said. With a tug on my braid's, she stepped back and closed her gate without a sound.

The darkness around her began to swallow her and the sound of my brothers. Her eyes glittered at me from the depths of the trees. "Don't underestimate des' men, Chile. They are much more dangerous than you tink." She was gone. Her voice said one last thing in a soft whisper that felt as if it were being spoken against my ear. "Nor, yo' self."

Then she was really gone and her voice with her, leaving me to face whatever was out there. My crew came up and pushed me toward my bike. The wind picked up, sending a chill racing up my spine. The sky began to darken around us as we sped toward the industrial park. Further and further east we rode until my apartment and safety was out of sight.

Chapter 17

At the industrial park it had become full dark and, as Enrique pointed out, there was actively still going on, but it had definitely slowed down. We'd met at the Convenience Store and counted heads. There were thirty of us and still no signs of the team Jamal and David were being so mysterious about. We'd set-up a command post of sorts at the front of the building with an old crate as a table and a brown paper bag ripped down it's sides, where we planned the assault on the warehouse a.k.a. fortress. An argument had started and we'd been at it for about five minutes now. Actually it wasn't we, it was them. You know them. The guys. Yeah. Jamal and David were arguing with Enrique and his friends. The machismo of the two opposing groups completely pushed the rest of us to the back, where we quite happily organized a rescue without either group's input. We'd also formulated a plan "b".

Things were going fine until the argument ended abruptly, causing every head involved in the real planning session to look up in surprise. What we saw scared me near to death. Jamal and David slid down the embankment to east of the brightly lit doorway. There was still a slow trickle of activity as the last few boxes and crates were being shuttled from the building.

Ro's eyes must have mirrored the disbelief in my own, and the poor twins looked ready to pass out from shock. Then that Enrique came over and had the nerve to stare down at me.

"Su Cuñado decided to go in on his own." his friends started their nudging and laughing. "So, I told him to go ahead and me and my boys would be sure to rescue him when he started yellin' for his ma'ma."

I stood slowly pulling Roberta to my side to keep her from telling Enrique off, not that he didn't deserve it for acting like an incredible jerk. I had something much better in mind. I smiled at him. He flinched. See, I told you he wasn't stupid.

"Thank you for all your help, and like I said, I owe you one." He started to give me his superior smile. Foolish man. "Let me give you a little something as a deposit." I moved closer and I guess he thought I was going to smooch him or something because his eyes glazed over and went out of focus. That's when I touched his shoulders and brought my knee up between his legs so hard that I heard generations of his family crying out in pain. He tried too late to protect his jewels, so I gave him a little bit of a push so the ground could lend him the support he obviously needed.

Without a backward glance at him, I signaled the others to fall into step behind me, which they did with only the slightest pause to survey my handiwork.

The brush around the incline obscured us from the people below while giving us a perfect view of everything going on down there.

"Girl, one day your temper is going to get us all killed." I shushed Ro. just as the brush, a few feet away, started to jump and shake. We looked on in surprise, then the group of bushes began to yell and grunt. Next thing anyone knew, David and Jamal were being pushed out of the shrubbery by the same two thugs who'd followed us and who we'd also followed.

Jamal walked in front with his head down, but that David had the nerve to look up. Right at us. Then they pushed him through the door where he vanished.

"Idiots, Idiots, Idiots." I guess I would have gotten really loud if Ro. and Paula hadn't reached out to me at the same time, jerking me out of whatever trance those idiots had put me in. I gripped the hands on my shoulders before turning around to face the friends who'd gathered for no other reason than to help us. Friends who were finally beginning to understand that this wasn't a game, this was real. Still, no one left. A small voice toward the front said, "What we gonna do now, Keisha?" I smiled at the "we". Because I knew it really meant me and what good does it do to fight about that now. So, I didn't take offense. I'd made this bed, so I had to sleep in it.

"I don't know what your smilin' at crazy girl. But you better hurry up." That was from Ro.

"Plan B". I signaled everyone closer and we went back into the quickest huddle in history.

Chapter 18

I n the warehouse, Jamal and David were both blinded for a couple of moments after stepping from darkness into the flood lights inside. After much blinking, the dots slowly faded from their eyes. There was nothing in the way of furnishings to be seen. The whole building was empty except for a few stray boxes and a cluster of people maybe about ten or fifteen yards from the door.

The two didn't have time to talk. It wouldn't have made any difference. Jamal was numb. He'd done something stupid and now both he and David were in a load of trouble with no way out. David, on the other hand, was irrepressibly optimistic. Keisha would save them. He didn't know how, but he believed.

Hazy figures dissolved into a very pale man in a blazingly white suite; a shriveled - up little man with brown hair and a suit to match, along with two amazingly - similar couples, Lewis's both. Except, one of the couples were buppies and the other were the scientists parents of Jamal Lewis.

"Jamal!" burst from the real Mrs. Doctor Lewis. Her son jumped, then flew into her arms in a way that reminded her of the baby he used to be. She curled herself around him, and his father held onto them both from behind. No words. Just warmth.

"Touching. Really." the cold voice said. The family unfolded itself, but continued to hold on to each other. A silk, lace-ruffled handkerchief dabbed delicately beneath The Man's icy eyes.

"And while happy family reunions just do something to me." The scrap of fabric was busily folded and stowed away inside an inner pocket. "But, young man, you have something that belongs to me." A small movement of his head and the goons snatched Jamal from the arms of his parents. David had been hovering on the side of the Lewises, feeling alone. A big brown hand descended on his shoulder and pulled him close to the side of Mr. Lewis. The arm gave him a squeeze, and he looked up into eyes that had no reason to be reassuring but were, just the same.

"Child, what are you two doing here?"

"We're here to save you, Sir." Eyes widened and met those of his wife, who grabbed his arm. A ghost of a smile danced across her eyes before a cloud of dread pushed the glow away. Before he could stop himself, David found himself blurting out what he felt sure would be reassuring.

"Don't worry, Mrs. Lewis." The Doctors looked from him to their son who was being questioned between the two burly thugs who were physically very similar to the two who'd tortured them hours earlier. They expected nothing less than to give their lives to keep the same from happening to Jamal. Most of their hope was gone, they wouldn't crush David's.

"Certainly, honey."

David's optimism was not to be denied even when the pale man got louder and louder. The man, then, drew back his hand as if to slap Jamal's face. Jamal was shaking his head "no" as loud as his mouth was shouting it.

Then, two loud bangs and a polite voice interrupted with, "Excuse me have you seen a cat?"

The group turned to find two angelic-faced girls standing in the door. One olive-complexioned with a single long braid and one cinnamon brown with many braids pulled back from her face. The latter dropped the brick behind her in embarrassment with a solid thunk.

David looked up at the Lewis's with a big grin. "Keisha's here." And the Lewis's snapped their mouths closed and fervently began to pray.

Chapter 19

You know, no one believed that plan "B" would work, no one but me. It seemed like the boldest of moves would be the one that should make everything come together. Time and my position of power had been the only reason Ro. and I were standing in the door. Suddenly, I was having serious second thoughts.

I'd just dropped the brick behind me, which was our signal to the guys on the hill. They started moving quietly into position. I didn't turn to check, I could feel them as surely as I felt the light breeze playin' with the hairs on my arm. One of our big burly friends headed toward us while the other continued to hold Jamal in one beefy fist.

"Maybe this wasn't such a good idea?" The thug reached us, taking one on each side and jerking us toward the rest of the captives. Ro. looked around his big ole' gut at me and managed to say, "Girl, if we make it through this we're going to have a long talk!" She was jerked around to face the front.

We stopped, standing in front of a long tall drink of water. Or should I say milk? From his head to toe there was nothin' but white. I don't mean what other people call white because that's only a paler shade of brown or even pink. No, this guy was like paper. He looked down on the two of us with ice caps where his eyes should be. For the very first time in my life I began to believe in true evil. I knew him. Maybe not from here, we had been enemies in another time and place, as we would be in this time and forever. He knew there was something. He wasn't sure exactly what, but he knew something was going on. He shook his head in an attempt to dispel the strangeness that is me. Poor man. I have that effect on everyone.

"Well, what have we here?" He smiled in that condescending way that many older people use when they speak to younger people. Our henchman eased toward his boss and tried to whisper. "Ah, beggin' your pardon, Mr. Dupree, Sir. But, these two girls what was with these two boys out at the house the other day." He pointed toward the Lewis's with an elbow. I guess he didn't trust us enough to remove a hand. His tone said much more than his words ever could. Beware! Beware!

But that fool Dupree was much too smart to listen to an uneducated roughneck. "Why, my word," He smiled down at Ro. and me. "These sweet little girls supposedly beat you up and escaped from two well-armed rough types like yourselves?"

His smile turned colder, if that's possible. "Release them." Two words. That's all it took and Ro. and myself were in striking distance.

"But, Mr. Dupree.." started the guy who still held onto Jamal, more for moral support for himself rather than any need to restrain Jamal.

A pale, manicured hand halted his stammered speech, "where was?", he pretended to have forgotten what he was going to say. "Oh, yes, My dear young ladies, perhaps you could do me a favor.' He looked hopefully at the two of us. His crocodile eyes actually sparkled. "This young man," waving the same slow hand in Jamal's direction, "took something that belongs to me." His face became sad and regretful. Oh yeah, he was good. I was nearly moved to feeling sorry for him. No, Not, uh, uh.

"We'd just began to inquiring as to the whereabouts of said property." He smiled brightly at me. "When you arrived." Jamal began to shake his head trying to get my attention. I suppose he was trying to tell me not to admit to anything having to do with the papers we'd left at my house. Didn't he know who I was? I knew how to handle myself. After all, hadn't I come up with this glorious plan "B".

"You mean the papers we found in Jamal's house in the safe downstairs?" There were gasps and strange "Homer Simpson" like noises. Ro. was staring at me like I'd grown a second head or something. But this Samuel guy was eating it up.

"That's wonderful, darling." He was almost clapping his hands with joy. He actually pinched my check. Although the coldness never left his eyes. "Now, my dear, where are my papers?" Jamal's head was bowed in misery. Everyone else wore similar expressions. Everyone except David, he just grinned and that fool actually winked. We were definitely going to have a very long talk after this mess was over. That is, if we make it out alive.

My turn to smile. "Well, they could be just about anywhere now couldn't they?" I shook off the hand of the big potato-head guy, that had found it's way back on my arm, off. And put my hands on my hips. Stepping forward I added a little head and finger action. "They could be in de Ocean. They could be in de fire." I paused and touched the finger I'd been waving to my lips, consciously imitating the pale creature standing two feet away.

"I could tell you anything. But truth is," dramatic pause, "Those papers are somewhere you ain't never going to find them." I snapped my finger and showed him my back as I turned to find my place at the side of the Neanderthal.

Now I know your going to find this hard to believe. I mean I find it hard to believe and it happened to me. That man put his hand on me. Yes, he did! He grabbed my arm and swung me around to face him.

"Listen, you silly little cow, either you return to me what is rightfully mine, or I'll kill every last one of your friends." He glanced over his shoulder. "That includes parents as well as their doubles." The impostors, who had been unconcerned up to that point, suddenly found things to be most fascinating.

I'm not sure what he expected, but I know it wasn't what he got. Something changed inside me. "I don't know about where you come from, but where I come from you don't use language like that unless you're ready to fight." Ro. yelled, "no," but it was too late. I was in horse stance and I delivered the most perfect front instep kick I've ever thrown in my life.

Everything went into slow mo' and I watched surprise and pain chase themselves across Smart - boy's face. A face that was no longer pale, but a fiery red.

I had a short while to notice the color change before the lights went out.

Chapter 20

'm told the lights were out for no more than a couple of minutes. I say I'm told because there hadn't been a black-out. Unless you count the one in my head. A walking wall had clubbed me from behind. If you think about it you could almost take it as a compliment. Almost.

I blinked my eyes quickly trying to stop the dots from making more little patterns. They cleared enough for me to see the pair of sturdy knees right in front of my face. I found myself with my head in Dr. Mrs. or Mrs. Dr. Lewis's lap, and Ro. leaning over me anxiously. I was confused about why I was on my side until I tried to sit-up. They'd tied my arms together behind my back. Mrs. Dr. had to help me to sit up.

Once again I was the center of a huddle, consisting of the Lewis's both real and fake, and David and Ro. I'm not sure about the motive of the copy-cat Lewis's, but I guess they wanted protection. I didn't have time to worry about them. All my attention had to be on the man.

He really should have taken the time to change his suit. Red really didn't go with his snowy white motif. They'd scrounged up a chair from somewhere and he was reclined on it. The picture of relaxation. Except of course for his very red face and the muscle spasms that rocked him every few minutes until he could gain a short-lived control. His people were arrayed almost in the same sort of pattern that we captured folks were in. Ironically, they seemed to be more afraid than any of us. I suppose they weren't as stupid as I'd thought. I'd been knocked unconscious and I could actually feel the lump beginning to form on the back of my head. It throbbed with every beat of my hear. I should have been scared quiet. But I wasn't. Grandma used to say that I was a child who didn't believe fat meat was greasy. I guess she was right.

"Who are you anyway? And why did you want the Lewis's?" Everyone shushed me loudly and Ro. actually covered my mouth with her hand. I was just as surprised as they were to hear myself saying anything, let alone demanding an explanation. I bit her anyway. Her "Ow!" was followed by a very bad word in Spanish which everyone in the room of course understood. I giggled. It seemed to relax everyone except the person from who I'd demanded a response.

"How very vulgar." His statement was meant to make us all feel worthless. I suppose if he hadn't had a fit after pronouncing the last word it would have worked, but his twitching only made me laugh again, louder than before.

The metallic clang of his chair flipping onto it's side stopped me in mid - chuckle better than anything short of a nuclear war could. He'd propelled himself to a spot directly in front of me. Although, he was definitely out of kicking range.

"You silly little girl," He pause to twitch, "you don't have enough sense to even be afraid, do you?' twitch, twitch. He thought he knew so much. I was so scared that I was only holding it together enough not to wet my pants. Oh yeah, I was scared, but he would never be the one to see it. He started pacing until he realized that that just increased the amount of twitching. A "snap" of his fingers sent the little brown man hurrying forward with his chair. For the first time, I was able to make eye contact with this sad person, as he held the chair for twitchy. His eyes were so sad. But there was something else as well - a nameless something.

The red-faced, little man settled himself in the chair. Yeah, I know I've already described him as being tall, but he'd begun to come apart and he actually started to shrink to me.

"Samuel Dupree," he said with a twist of his lips. "At your service." His shoulders spasmed, pushing him against the backrest of his chair, as he tried to pretend that it had been his intention all along. We edged close to each other. It reminded me of library reading circle. Although, I was pretty sure this story's author didn't have a happy ending planned. Pale eyes went unfocused as he began to unfold his plot.

"Oh, such an excellent scheme really.' He smiled wistfully at the ceiling at something that he alone could see. "The perfect plan," He nearly sighed with joy. " An obscure formulae found accidentally by two absent-minded scientists." He spared a fond smile for the Doctors Lewis.

"I won't bore you with the particulars of the formulae. Actually, the formula itself means very little in my plan." The two Doctors shifted in confusion. They were remembering the pain and terror they'd endured through many hours of work creating the mixture spelled out in their available data.

"Oh, yes, I needed the re-creation of your notes. That was indeed very important, but what it created is absolutely worthless." He began to chuckle at the expressions on our faces. "You don't believe I would go through all of this for something that meant nothing. That's what made my plan fool proof. No one would believe that it didn't do whatever I said it would. Eventually, they'd understand they'd been tricked, but until that time came my pockets would have been overflowing." Once again, his face took on the same dreamy quality as before when he imagined the wealth. In the silence of all of us thinking our own thoughts, a welcome sound could be heard faintly in the distance.

"Oh, Dios Mio" Ro. crossed herself and tears rolled down her face. They were tears of relief because the sound was unmistakably police sirens. Even the Doctors Lewis were hugging each other in relief and joy. They were also happily squeezing the breath from David who'd been sitting between the two of them.

But I couldn't rejoice, I was watching Samuel Dupree. The sound of those sirens did what all his attempted self-control hadn't been able to do just moments before. It stopped his spasms and removed the unbecoming color from his face so that he once again matched his immaculate suit. As I watched, his face lost all animation, until he was again the beast I'd met just an hour or so before, although it felt much more like days to me. I continued to watch him, he began to watch me. The quality of my stillness drew Ro.'s attention, and she went to move closer to my side. Without looking at her I pushed her further away from me. It was not more than a couple of feet, but it was the best I could do without taking my eyes from the battle I was fighting.

Samuel smiled and opened his jacket exposing a beautiful brocade waist coat, vest to you and me. The pattern was very involved and drew the eye to the shifting swirls on the white satin. His hand moved across my line of sight. That long, delicate hand pulled from his hip a small caliber pistol made of..yeah..you guessed it, white gold. It glinted and gleamed at me until I could see the small mouth of it. Without thought, I began to gather myself. Silently, yet swiftly, I called the wind to do my bidding. But, before I could focus let alone harness any of it, that deadly work of art twitched slightly upward. My eyes followed it's motion and I looked into the face of evil on earth. Instead of being afraid, I felt fired up. I had a minute or so before he pulled the trigger. Besides, he owed me at least one witty remark before he became Dirty Harry.

I continued to pump myself up with power. By the time I'd finished, the room felt electric with my power. Wind whirled and twisted with me as it's center. Everyone in my vicinity had moved away, everyone but Samuel and that hard-headed Roberta Gabriella Rodriguez. She was a little behind and to the left of me.

"What is going on here?" The gun wavered a bit with the first glimpse of uncertainty Samuel Dupree had experienced. I had a few extra seconds, "Move" I screamed at Ro. She jumped, and I knew she was scared but her arms were crossed over her chest, just as my unbound ones were over mine. She wasn't moving. No prob. I had plenty of energy to spare. It was easy. I focused and the wind that had been moving aimlessly gathered and became a funnel. With a thought, I sent it after my best friend. It raged until it touched her tennis shoes then it became a gentle breeze that danced and played with her braid and the legs of her from the floor and began to move her to the door and my friends waiting there.

"Excuse me." halted everything, Ro., my heart, breathing, the whole nine yards. She'd only gone about ten feet or so. Far enough away from me I hoped, but not nearly close enough to the door as I would have liked.

One quick breath and I turned back to him. And the gun. He smiled and adjusted his jacket, "where was I? Oh, yes." The gun was back in place and my heart knew I had the time between two blinks to save my life. "Everything is a joke for you young woman." He chuckled, "Not so funny now is it?" He fired.

I shielded and the bullet ricocheted off the crystal case that partially surrounded me. Sparks flew in a shower from the impact and the bullet angled toward my left. Toward Ro. my eyes followed it's path, I couldn't look away. She jumped then crumpled just like on television. Except there was no camera and I knew she wouldn't jump up when someone yelled cut. An animal somewhere started screaming and didn't stop until I was at Ro.'s side, then I realized the sound had been coming from me.

"Oh God, Oh God, Ro! Ro!" I couldn't bring myself to touch her. I couldn't check to make sure she was alive. I was numb and clueless. As if from a long distance away, I felt pain as Samuel wound his hand in my braids and dragged my nearly limp body from the ground. I didn't care. If Ro. wasn't all right nothing else mattered. We passed Jamal and David, but they were just blurry, shadowed figures. I couldn't see or feel anything.

The arm holding the gun to my back shook slightly and it finally registered with me that my life was still in danger. I tried to focus but I could barely make my legs move. Left, right, left, right.

We stepped from the light of the building into the dark night. Sirens blared nearer, but not as near as the white limousine with doors open and thugs standing by with guns drawn. This scene reminded me that this was more important than what happened to me or even to Ro. This man was evil.

And I was the only thing standing between him and success, but I was acting like a baby. In my mind, my mother's voice came to me the way it did in martial arts training when sparring was getting rough.

"Girl, put you chin down, plant your feet, and go for what you know!"

That's exactly what I did, planted my feet, which shocked Samuel and caused him to run into me; which put him right where I wanted him.

"Wah." was all he managed before both my hands came up covering the one he still had gripped in my braids. I dipped to the left taking his hand with me and pulling him off balance and into my control. Next, I moved right and slightly behind him. He screamed and his hand, amazingly enough, let go of my hair and the other dropped that pretty little gun. I could have stopped there, but vengeance required more of me. His arm held him immobile. I gave him a extra little twist which succeeded in making him bend almost double. That move put him in perfect position for me to kick him as hard as I could in the face Blood gushed from his nose and I let him go to fall with a satisfying splat to the ground.

Joy rushed into me and finally I was able to gather the wind. It lifted around me and swirled my braids. My arms raised as the wind sang in my blood for the first time and I looked at the men holding their guns forgotten by their sides. Fear raged in their faces. Fear of me.

Their fear connected the three of us and I saw myself through their eyes and I didn't like what I saw. I let go of the wind. All my energy deserted me and I landed on my butt near the awakening Samuel Dupree.

"You wittle witch," He couldn't speak clearly, because I had broken his nose. I believe if he hadn't been afraid of my breaking something else he probably would have tried for his gun which was closer to me than him.

"Skoot her, you fools, skoot her!" First Bob, then Rick aimed their guns at me. (I'd learned their names while there'd still been a connection between us.)

"Now!" I screamed at the top of my lungs. A half-circle of lights surrounded us. Half a second passed in silence until something came flying out of the night and landed with a wet sound on top of the limo. Bob had flinched away from the missile. when nothing else happened, he tested the white stuff carefully with a finger. He squeezed it, sniffed it and touched it to his tongue.

"Flour," he said in surprise. Both he and Rick began to laugh. That's probably why the next two bombs landed in their half-opened mouths. Except these bombs weren't flour. These were shaving cream and toilet paper. From then on, the air was full of flying packages of destruction, some of which even landed on me. I didn't have any energy left to get out of the way, so I just curled up in a ball on the ground and tried to stay out of the way as my plan worked itself out. And work it did. Those missiles beat down on my enemies and Bob and Rick were soon on their knees. I didn't get a chance to be relieved, because it occurred to me there was someone else who I hadn't heard from for some time. I shifted my position in time to see Samuel pick up his little gun. He grinned evilly and without a word began to squeeze the trigger.

I closed my eyes and prayed. Prayed without words. I just called out for help with everything I had left. Time passed. Too much time so I opened my eyes to check the scene and found the mousy brown man, standing over a very unconscious Samuel Dupree, with a big stick in his hand. The mousy brown man smiled and I felt his spirit beginning to change. To heal. With a nod he dropped the stick and walked into the night.

"Yeah, ah.,a," as running feet came out from the building behind me. The yell came from the circle of lights. A large group detached themselves from the dark and came charging. Long sticks, short skirts and big legs.

LaShara, the captain of the field hockey team, gave orders and Bob and Rick were face down on the pavement with their hands tied behind their backs almost before they had a chance to think about what was happening.

Jamal and David appeared one on each side of me. Jamal sat down close. He didn't say anything. He didn't even look at me. I don't know what I would have done if he had. David continued on to stand beside LaShara who smiled at him and tweaked his cheeks. I looked at Jamal. He grinned, "She likes him." He shrugged "That's why the team is here." I giggled, then I laughed, then I screamed, then cried. Jamal's arms went around me and I fell against him and let the tears come. I cried from fear and pain, but more than anything else I cried because of guilt and shame. I'd thought I was "all that" and my pride had cause so much pain. Hubris. It went on and on."

The sirens had come to a halt and the crooks were taken into custody without my being aware of any of it. I'd stopped crying by that time, and Jamal shifted uncomfortably. The hair on the back of my neck stood up. And I removed my head from his shoulder and saw shiny black shoes. My eyes followed the tip of the shoes to the cuff of dark blue trousers well-pressed and with a darker line that I couldn't see but knew was there. Up, up, dark hands rested on hips. All the way to the top where my mother's face stared down at me with rage that spoke loudly of corporal punishment.

She moved slightly, and an even larger figure stepped nearer to her and into my line of sight. It was the last thing I saw for quite some time. You see, my PaPa Rodriquez had found us, and his face reminded me that Ro. had been shot. His face was the last straw. So for the second time in my life I went out like a light.

Five Weeks Later

It's been weeks since that mess was finally over. Mom and Pop, after hugging me so hard I could barely breath, had decided that a month's restriction was sufficient punishment. I was only allowed to go as far as the top of the stairs. No T.V., or telephone. To be honest, I didn't mind, I had a lot to do anyway.

Roberta's shoulder healed perfectly, she actually seems to be quite proud of her "battle" scar. She'd come over the day after she'd left the hospital. And I told her as much about the things I could do as would get her to leave me alone. We'd cried over her wound and I had told her that I would never use this whatever again. It had done a lot of good, but had caused so much pain at the same time.

Samuel and his henchman had been take to England by Interpol. Apparently, what he had done to the Lewis's was nothing compared to the things he'd done over there or still planned to do. The last I'd seen of him was in the police car. His eyes, still cold, had sent me a clear message and I knew he and I weren't finished. We would meet again.

Jamal and David come over all the time now. They've actually become part of our misfits' crew, and the rest of us can't imagine a time when they weren't with us. We play, run, ride bikes and laugh. All of the usual things we'd done before. But now there was silences, especially from me. We'd been changed. We were still kids but we'd experienced evil unlike anything we'd known before. Not adults, but not completely kids either. None of us talk about it, at least, I don't. I can't speak for the others.

David decided that he wanted to have Roberta as his girlfriend. But Ro. told him in no uncertain terms that he wasn't her type. And once the swelling had gone down in his eye he admitted that she was probably right.

Jamal and I look, and are more gentle with each other than with the other guys. But we silently agreed that someday when we're both ready, our relationship would change. Until then, we were both happy being friends.

The sun still sets over the ocean with blazes of reds, golds and oranges and as I sit on the third step from the bottom and look toward the west. The beauty of it makes me cry. My friends have come and they are dragging me down the steps to go get ice cream cones. We pass Mrs. G.'s house and she's sitting in her rocker stroking Hat's head and humming quietly to herself. Our eye's meet and she quietly sends me her love and affection and concern.

My friends have gotten ahead of me and yell at me to catch up. Jamal comes back and grabs the hand that had been resting on Mrs. Gutierrez's fence and pulls me on.

I waved goodbye to her, but as I turned away, my hand still in Jamal's, her voice speaks softly in my head. "You have a little time child, a very little time. Destiny will call you back and all your choices will be gone." I shivered in the warmth of the night and gave Jamal's hand a squeeze. He smiled at me with a question in his eyes. I smiled back, laughed, dropped his hand and ran toward Roberta and the gang with Jamal close behind.

I will enjoy these days, I guess I know that Mrs. G. is right. I only have a little time. Catching up with my friends, I smack Ro. really hard on the butt and scream, "you're it!" as I run into the night.

Mrs. G.'s Epilogue

Yeah, Chile, I watched her through this bit o' trauma. She handled herself well. I got great hopes for dis' spirit chile o' mine. She feel de pain o' her little friend and blames herself for wot' happened to her. She dun' vowed never to do what she do best, that be talking and listenin' to da wind and moving and workin' in the lives of the people around her. She say it be too much power and responsibility for a chile or anyone else for dat' matter. She say she be a chile a while longer. My Keisha decided to live in denial for a time. But her momma came to see me and we don' had a meetin' of the minds. Between the two of us we'll cushion her while she heals. While she plays with her friends and goes to shows, we'll be there to support her when she needs it and to catch her when she falls.

She waved to me as she ran passed my gate. Hat rubbed against my leg, beggin' for a stroke. Pickin' her up, she meowed soulfully at Keisha.

"Don't worry Hat, she be all right. She just ain't a chile no more. I know it. Her momma know it. And I bet Keisha knows it, too, somewhere deep inside.

I looked up at the moon, my goddess, and sent a small adoration then I crossed myself and thanked de' Lord. But in my mind and heart I knew dat her time of peace would be short. Keisha's destiny was stronger than most and would not be denied.